SHATTERED

A Broadmoor Prep Academy Novel

LJ Byrne

Amazon

ISBN-13: 9798685720566

Cover design by: Canva.com
Images courtesy of Flaticon.com
Library of Congress Control Number: 2018675309
Printed in the United States of America

SHATTERED

PROLOGUE

This can't be right. The police surround the Kings' home. At a distance, I see my four boys, my Knights: Kai, Nate, Tristan, Eric. But they aren't smiling. They look... mad. That makes no sense. They're never mad at me. I want to run to them, but I'm too ashamed. I don't want them to know.

I tremble. There are too many people around, and I start to feel the panic rise in my throat. I'm vulnerable and afraid.

Shin puts his arm around my shoulder. If anyone else had touched me, I would have started screaming. "We need to go."

I look at him. He's been a constant my whole life, but right now I can't understand him or read him. "I don't get it. Where are we going?" I ask him. "Please, Shin, I want to go home." Tears come to my eyes. Where's my father?

Shin looks at me, his mouth tight. We're "Irish twins" – he's only a year older – so we've always been close. "I need you to be strong, Mina. Dad's dead." He walks me to a police car. "We're heading to the police station." He says it so emotionlessly that I'm sure he's wrong. But then I see Shin's eyes.

Dad's dead. The words echo inside me until I shake with horror. "No. No!" I know why Dad's dead. This is all my fault. I feel sick and the desire to have a hot bath is overwhelming. I try to make a run for it, screaming, "Daddy! Daddy, don't!" Shin grabs me.

I start crying. I want to run to Tristan and tell him I'm scared. Why is he standing so far away? Why are they all standing so far away? Do they know? My eyes find Tristan's and I can't move as my skin crawls. "Where's Mom? Mom? Mom!" I scream her name, trying to break from Shin's hold.

My brother opens the door to the police car. Am I being arrested? Have I done something wrong? What's happening? "We need to make a statement, Mina." Shin's shaking with the effort to be calm. "Get in the car. Don't make a fuss."

What? Why? And that's when I see Mom. She's covered in blood. Is she hurt? Why is she handcuffed? When she looks at me, her eyes are flat. "You should've kept your mouth shut, you stupid girl!" she hisses.

I flinch. My world collapses. I get told the police are taking us in until CPS can talk to us. As Shin helps me into the car, I meet Tristan's gray eyes. He mouths 'I hate you' as we leave. My world shatters in less than a day.

CHAPTER ONE

FIVE YEARS AGO...

In our neighborhood, everyone is rich, and everyone pretends to be happy. Then there's the four of us: Tristan, Eric, Kai, and me. We've been friends since we started at the same private school when we were five.

This is not a place where parents fawn over their children all the time. Some of us are pawns to use as bargaining chips. Others are merely manifestations of our parents' ambitions. A few are inconveniences. In a world of helicopter parents, our parents are a mix of lawnmowers with too much money.

First, it was me and Eric. Tristan wandered into our lives not long after. Kai was the last to join. We're friends out of necessity: wealth dictates us, need drives us. Our parents know each other. We go to the same parties. They expect us to date the same kind of girls. We go to the same private schools.

The house next to Tristan's is the smallest in the neighborhood, but it has the prettiest yard. It sold a month ago and now it looks like the new neighbors have arrived.

On the front lawn, someone has placed a blanket out, and a boy and a girl about our age are watching the movers. They're both dressed well, but they seem unusually serious as they look at the activity before them. The girl notices us first.

At twelve, I'm just starting to realize that girls are pretty; this girl is undeniably pretty. There's still a bit of baby fat in her cheeks, but her heart-shaped face shines through. The way she sits, you'd think she was a little doll with her legs tucked beneath her blue skirt and her small hands in her lap. Her brown eyes are wide and curious as she smiles at us shyly.

Tristan always acts like our unspoken leader. He steps up, nodding but not smiling at the two. "I'm Tristan King. I live in the house over there," he says, gesturing to the taller home. He introduces the rest of us. "Kai Reeves is the big guy. Eric Mansfield lives four houses away. Nate Remington."

The girl lowers her eyes, glancing at the boy next to her. But she isn't asking for permission or acting submissive. Her look clearly says *Introduce us*. The boy speaks up. "I'm Shin Steele. This is my little sister, Mina." He points to the Asian woman scolding the movers. "That's our mom." A man with blond hair pokes his head out of the window and looks down at us. Shin glances up with a grin. "Hey, Dad. Mom's terrorizing the movers."

Shin's father laughs, and it's not a laugh we often hear in our households. It's gentle and full of warmth. He has a kind face. Most of our dads are continually grumpy. "I'm jumping on a call." He nods at us. "Don't let your baby sister wander around if you go for a walk."

When he disappears, Mina's face scrunches. "I'm not a baby! You're only a year older!" She stands up, brushing her long hair back. Her eyes flicker over us. It's clear she's decided something. "Shin says our yard is too small to build a treehouse, but I disagree." Her voice is clear and precise and challenging.

I find myself grinning like an idiot. "I think you could build a treehouse." When I say that, her eyes sparkle.

"See, he agrees with me," Mina says with a triumphant look at her brother. "You can be my first new friends here."

I frown because her eyes are on Tristan and not me. I have to admit he seems dazzled by her, too. He's been watching her the entire time. "Do you have a plan for the treehouse?" Tristan asks her.

She grabs Tristan's hand and Kai's hand simultaneously, drawing them to the backyard. Shin sighs as he stands while his sister drags the two to the backyard, and we all follow. Her brother's sigh is full of affection and dismay.

Mina stops by one of the large trees on the property. "See? This has the right structure." She starts describing her idea of a treehouse, which sounds a lot more like a tiny castle. There's a small smile on Tristan's face as he listens to her detailed wishes. When she sees Eric walking around the tree, she engages him by pointing out where the *floors* of her treehouse would go.

"Now you've done it," Shin says to us. "She's gonna rope you in." His tone is light and full of laughter.

"Does she do this a lot?" I ask and Shin just smiles, shaking his head.

Shin puts his arm around his sister. They're close. "Be nice to them, little bug. They don't know what a taskmaster you are."

"It's called teamwork," Mina insists. "I'm not being bossy, am I?" We don't get a chance to answer before she winsomely asks, "Do you think we can have turrets, Eric?"

Eric thoughtfully nods as Mina grabs Kai's arm. "Help me up," she demands.

When Kai seems confused, she makes him loop his hands so she can use it to hoist herself up. I hear Shin warn her, but she ignores him as she kicks off her sandals and places a slender foot into Kai's hands. He immediately boosts her up as Eric comes over, thinking she might fall. Skillfully, she grabs the lower limb of the tree and lifts herself until she's perched on the limb.

Her legs dangle above our heads as she says, "If we can build up to that limb, we'd have a wonderful lookout. Don't you think, Nate?"

When she talks to me, I feel the heat rise in my face. "Yes, I think so."

"You climb like a monkey," Eric says to her, and I can tell he admires her already. No girl in this neighborhood would climb a tree like that.

"Just you four will have to do," Mina says. She sounds bossy, but I don't mind. "Aren't there girls in this neighborhood?"

"Yes," Kai says, speaking for the first time.
Tristan adds, "But none like you."
When she smiles, we all grin at her like idiots.

CHAPTER TWO

FIVE YEARS AGO…

This is the first time in years that I look forward to school. I normally hate school. Unlike Tristan and Nate, I'm not that smart. I'm great at sports and that's about it. No, the reason why school is better is because of a dark-haired girl who is attending with us. Shin is in eighth grade, but we've somehow looped him into our group along with Mina, who's come to rule the four of us. It just happened naturally.

Shin plays basketball, I play lacrosse, and Eric's the swimmer. Tristan and Nate also play lacrosse, but they aren't as good as I am. Basically, if it's a sport, I know how to conquer it. At Broadmoor Lower School, the feeder to Broadmoor Preparatory Academy, it's important to have a clique if you want to survive.

Since the seventh graders are in a different building, we enter our wing like we own it. Mina is sandwiched between me and Tristan. Eric and Nate guard our backs. We make it clear that Mina is with us. The students part as they eye the new girl in our midst.

It's with bitterness that I watch Tristan and Mina head to the accelerated math class. Eric and Nate are in science together, and I go to English on my own. I don't see any of them until right before lunch, but things don't go as planned.

The first thing I notice is Kimberly Moore snickering with her friends as they head to the lunchroom. She's only happy when she's hurting someone. That worries me. Then I hear faint weeping. I know that sound. I know who's upset.

I don't care that this is the girls' locker room. The sound propels me forward. I enter and find Mina curled into a ball. Her hair is messy, and some chunks of her hair are on the ground. *Someone cut her hair?!* The remaining girls don't do a thing to help Mina, but that doesn't stop them from screaming at me to leave.

"Out!" I roar back. My voice is deep due to a recent voice change. The girls scream and flee. With gentle hands, I touch Mina's shoulders. When her tear-stained face lifts, I see scratches on her neck and cheeks. Without hesitation, she flings herself at me, wrapping her thin arms around my neck and hiding her face in my shirt.

Mina is brave. She's a fighter. But right now, she turns to me for creature comfort.

I don't need to ask who hurt her. As much as I want to scream, I need to help Mina. I grab her things. With one arm around her waist, we stand up. A few more chunks of her hair fall to the ground. Kimberly will pay. I don't care if I get expelled. I don't care about anything other than making Kimberly pay.

At the nurse's, Mina refuses to tell the school who did this to her. There are no cameras in the locker rooms. The principal tries to explain that there is zero tolerance to bullying at the school, which I know is a lie. Money can buy forgiveness... and passing grades.

Shin bursts into the nurse's office with Tristan, Nate, and Eric. The nurse tries to keep them out, but Tristan *orders* her to stand down. For a few minutes, Shin and Mina whisper to each other. She shakes her head a few times. What is she telling him that she won't tell us?

Tristan's angry. He's not used to being defied by students. "Who did this?" His question to me is low and controlled.

"Kimberly," I whisper back. My friend's face changes, grows dark and scary. Most people are afraid of me when I'm mad because I'm big. But they really should fear Tristan. He has a mean streak.

Right now, our focus is Mina. Shin takes a pair of scissors and evens out the edges. All in all, Mina has a lot of hair and the shorter do looks good on her. She finishes the day out with us shadowing her constantly. When the day is over, Tristan tells me to make sure Mina gets home safely. I know Tristan's mom sends a car for him whenever he needs a ride. While I want to be part of Tristan's plan, I know that Tristan is giving me the most important task: making sure Mina is safe.

Mina and Shin don't ask questions about why I'm there and the others aren't, and I like that Mina trusts me so much. She rests against Shin but holds my hand.

"Thank you for saving me," she says to me, kissing my cheek.

It's a friendship kiss, that's all. But for some reason, my heart swells.

The next day, Kimberly Moore shows up with more than half her hair missing. Actually, she shows up wearing a wig. With a bit of cajoling, we get another student to yank the wig off and learn that she's practically bald. I don't ask how Tristan pulled it off. The Moore family has a lot of money. Whatever happened, Kimberly either isn't reporting the attack or her family doesn't care because they've been told it isn't important.

In the lunchroom, Mina sits in between Tristan and me. Her hair has been trimmed and layered. It goes past her shoulders and swings prettily when she turns her head. "You look nice," I tell her slowly, and she beams at me happily. She gives me the cookie on her plate. I see Eric frown at the gesture, but I just smile, enjoying the cookie.

Just then, Kimberly enters, her wig back on her head. The

students look at her. One kid throws a roll. Then another. Soon, Kimberly is being pelted with pieces of bread while the staff tries to intervene.

Mina stands up and runs to Kimberly, who's crying. Tristan and I are not far behind her. "Stop it!" Mina cries, covering Kimberly with her arms. "You don't have to be cruel to her!"

Our shock is obvious. Kimberly hurt her, yet Mina is defending her?

As soon as Tristan lifts his hand, the students go quiet. "You heard Mina. Stop!"

The students pull back as Kimberly lifts her teary face. She's not grateful. In fact, her face is full of hatred. Angrily, she pushes Mina away. I make a mean sound, lifting my hands. Kimberly looks at me fearfully before hissing at Mina, "I don't need help from you!" She flees the lunchroom.

"Come on," Tristan says, putting his arm around Mina. "Let's finish eating."

When Mina sits, Nate says, "You don't have to be nice to mean girls, Mina."

Mina's voice is clear. "Yes, I do. You never know if the kindness you give is the only kindness that person ever receives." She stops and looks shy. "I read that somewhere."

Under the table, Tristan's hand reaches for Mina's. He squeezes gently, staring at her.

When Mina shows up at my home that afternoon with Shin, I note that none of the other boys are with them. "Kai, can we talk?" Mina asks, extending her hand to me.

Shin pretends to open his book and read. That means he's only here because Mina wants to talk to me.

I always feel clumsy around her because she's so slight. I put her small hand in mine, and she leads me to the living room where we can talk privately. Shin doesn't follow us.

"I want to ask you something, but I don't want you to get mad at me," she says. She doesn't let go of my hand.

I want to laugh. I don't think there is anything she could do to make me angry. If I were braver, I'd sit her on my lap. But I'm not that brave. "I don't think I could ever be angry with you."

"Kai. Are you struggling to read?" When she looks at me, there isn't pity. Her eyes are clear and soft as she waits for me to respond.

I can't breathe for a moment. I wait for the taunts. *Stupid black kid can't read.* I hide it behind my athleticism. Enough money and enough talent can buy your grades at Broadmoor.

"Oh, Kai, don't be ashamed." She moves to sit right next to me. "I know it's not the same, but I don't know how to swim. I know Eric is the swimmer, but I'm too scared to ask him. Do you think you'd teach me to swim if I show you how to read?"

When I stammer out an excuse, she shakes her head. "I won't tell anyone, Kai. Not even Shin. Just you and me." She bites her lip. "I've been read about dyslexia. I can't be sure, but it's not uncommon. I think we can help each other. Will you help me?" I nod. "Will you let me help you?" I briefly hesitate. I nod again. "It'll be just between you and me." She hooks our pinkies together and leans against my shoulder. "Thank you for trusting me."

I know then that Mina owns a piece of my heart, and I don't ever want it back. I give it to her freely and willingly even if it means I'll never have hers.

CHAPTER THREE

FOUR YEARS AGO...

With four willing accomplices, Mina's treehouse – a castle, really – comes together beautifully. We cheat by hiring someone to put a good deal of it together, but the special touches – the lookout tower, the mounted water guns – that's all us.

It's an awkward time. We still play like we did last year, but our bodies are changing. Mina's taller, her legs longer, and she has curves that didn't exist before. We notice. I notice. Sometimes, when I'm around her, I can barely think straight. We still hang out with Mina and Shin a lot, but there are times when the four of us wander alone to talk about... girls. And honestly, more than once, the conversation goes back to how awesome Mina is.

Mina is both accessible and forbidden. Shin scowls at us when he catches us staring at Mina far too long. At Tristan's pool, we stare at Mina in her swimsuit. If she notices, she never says anything. She treats us equally with affection.

But Sean, Tristan's asshole older brother, mocks us. He thinks he's super cool because he's almost seventeen. There are few people Mina doesn't like, and I know she doesn't like him. His jokes are crude, and the way he looks at girls bothers me.

Sometimes I get mad at the other guys. In the pool, Mina turns to Kai when she's scared. He's the only one who she trusts in the deep end of the pool. Considering I'm the best swimmer, she should turn to me, right?

Then there's Nate. When Mina needs to talk or is worried, she turns to Nate. When we're eating or walking, she likes to be with Tristan. We all notice that Tristan holds her hand when we watch movies together.

As for me? Mina talks to me about art. We go for walks looking at the colors and textures in nature. She lets me sketch her, sitting still for long periods so I can sketch the texture of her hair or the way her fingers rest in her lap. Sometimes, when she's struggling with writing, we sit together and talk until I inspire her.

One hot summer day, Mina arms her water guns and attacks us from above. Tristan and Kai retaliate with water balloons, scaling her fortress to have their revenge. Nate turns traitor, using a mini catapult to attack us.

Mina, with her usual dexterity and grace, climbs out on a limb to slide down the rope to escape, the ribbon in her hair coming free and falling on a branch. Squealing with triumph, she grabs Nate as they locate the water balloon stash.

Tristan is the first down, and I'm right behind him. Before Nate can arm himself properly, I've wrestled him to the ground while Tristan wraps himself around Mina. They fall back to the ground, Tristan pinning Mina under him. Except for Mina, we all freeze. Tristan's gray eyes are wide as he looks at laughing, breathless Mina, his face inches from hers. Kai makes an odd sound.

"What's going on out here?" Euna Steele's voice is like icy water. "Mina, look at you. You're not a child anymore! I come out and find you dirty like a savage!"

Mina sobers, her dark eyes suddenly somber. Mina's mother never speaks kindly to Mina. We're used to it, but hearing it in person is upsetting. Tristan immediately lifts himself off her, helping Mina to her feet. She's gloriously muddy. She doesn't look savage – she looks alive. There's something wild and wonderful about her that her mother doesn't understand. "I'll go inside to change, Mom," Mina says quietly, the light in her eyes dimming.

"More laundry for me," Euna says, sniffing. She looks at all of us and smiles. "Well, say hello to your parents for me."

"I don't like her," Nate whispers as we wait for Mina to return.

Tristan doesn't say anything, but he's frowning. Is he thinking about Mina beneath him or about Mina's mother?

I look up at the ribbon in the tree. I should get it back for Mina to make her smile. Climbing up the tree quickly, the others ignore me as they mutter about Mina's mother.

The ribbon is just out of reach so I'm forced to edge out along the limb. As I grab the ribbon, my feet, slightly muddy from the ground, slips on the wet bark. I don't remember falling – just the slip and the sudden pain when I land on the ground. The guys come running. At first, I don't think it's too bad until the pain balloons in my left arm. I suck in my breath.

"Don't move!" Tristan snaps, his eyes wide with alarm.

"Eric!" Mina's voice makes me seek her out.

In clean jeans, she doesn't care about the dirt as she sends Nate in to call an ambulance while kneeling next to me. Her hands shake a little when she pushes my damp hair back to look at me. Her hair swings down in a dark curtain.

"Listen to me, Eric," she says softly. "Your skin feels cold. You're pale. I think you're going through a little shock. Kai, get a towel or blanket." Her fingers dance over my left arm, not touching but sensing the injury.

Dazed and in pain, I whisper, "You should become a doctor." All she is doing is comforting me, so I don't know why I say that.

"Stay with me, Eric," she urges me gently. Tristan kneels beside her, his hand on her back. "What happened?"

"I wanted to get the ribbon for your hair," I say softly. "I wanted to make you happy."

A genuine smile forms on her face. "You make me happy. All of you. That's why we're friends."

I want to ask Tristan why he touches her so much. "Mina,"

I gasp, as pain shoots through me when I try to move. When her hand touches my cheek, I focus on her face. "I want to draw you like this, leaning over me. Don't leave, okay?"

"I wouldn't ever leave," she promises. "You're my Knights."

I blink. She's created a name for us?

"That makes you our queen," Tristan says. "Don't you agree, Eric?"

"Always," I say. "Mina, you'll always be our queen."

Mina laughs. She begins to sing *I'll Be There* so that I must focus to hear her. In the distance, I hear the sirens. I know adults are surrounding me, but all I see and hear is Mina and the promise of our friendship.

CHAPTER FOUR

THREE YEARS AGO...

My hands shake. Dammit. I don't want to appear nervous. It's the summer before we enter high school. Broadmoor Prep Academy. Every four years, a new wave of kids becomes the reigning rulers of the school. They pick names for themselves: the Kings, the Aces, the Rooks. Right now, the Aces are on their way out. The Knights are their natural successor. But it won't be just the Knights. Mina is part of our power. She unifies us.

But that's not the reason why I'm pacing in front of her window. Kai and I started fighting again over Mina. So far, we've managed to keep the fighting away from her, but I'm sure she senses the tension. No matter what we feel, there's one Mina and we don't want to share her romantic affections. It's not just Kai, though. Eric and Nate give Mina the same look Kai does. They seem less willing to act on their feelings, though. I need to take the initiative first.

I grab a small pebble and throw it at Mina's window. When I see her shadow, I wonder if she knows it's me before she opens her curtains. Her hair is in a braid over her shoulder, and her small smile tells me she's happy to see me. She's down in an instant, coming out barefoot onto her screened back porch. She lets me in wearing a tank and a pair of sleep shorts.

Lately, all I can think about is the way she smells when she's close. She uses this pineapple-coconut shampoo and her hair soaks up the scent like crazy.

"People will start to talk if you keep running over here at night," she teases, her eyes sparkling. I want to believe they shine in a special way for me.

My heart pounds, but I shrug, trying to appear calm. "I don't care what people say. It's always us against everyone else, right?"

I try not to focus on the way her tank moves when she breathes. I don't think she's wearing a bra. "What's going on, Tristan?" Her question is soft but perceptive. "You have a mark on your cheek." She reaches out to brush the bruise with her fingers.

Mina appreciates honesty, so the best thing to do is be honest. "Who do you like best? Me or Kai?" I ask. I grab her hand, my thumb on her wrist. I can feel the pulse of her heart. I swear it's beating hard like mine.

Her dark eyes stare at me strangely. "There isn't one of you that I like better. What are you really asking?"

I let her hand go. When she remains silent, I stand and pace. "Kai and I are fighting. We're fighting over you, Mina. I've already made Eric and Nate back off, but Kai is too stubborn. We'll be in high school in a few months. When we go there, I don't want other guys to come after you. Other schools feed into Broadmoor Prep." When I look at her, she's pale and oddly quiet. My hopes sink, but I've already gone too far. "Mina, I like you more than a friend. I'm not saying I'm ready to make out or anything. You know, unless you want to." That comes out badly. "I want it so the other Knights know it's you and me. That you feel things for me, too."

I wish she would say something. Mina's usually an easy read, but right now I don't have a clue what she's thinking. Finally, she says, "If I pick one of you, it'll change everything." She averts her head, her body still in the dark. Finally, after a few minutes, she says, "But even if I don't, the change will still happen." She takes a deep breath – don't look, Tristan! – and her hand rubs her neck gently. "I don't want something like this to come between us."

She's not going to pick any of us. She doesn't want me at all. I misread everything. Panic and despair mix inside my stomach. Should I leave? Should I laugh?

She stands up and comes over to me, pressing her cool hand against my hot cheek. "When I first saw you, you were the most incredible boy I'd ever seen. I don't want to hurt Kai or Nate or Eric. They mean so much to me. All of you are my best friends." She sighs.

I want to be more than friends. Bitterness coats my tongue.

"But you're more than that. I don't know why, but it's always been you. You make me feel... alive."

What did she say? I can hardly breathe. "Are you... You're picking me?" When she nods, I spin her. I should feel bad for Kai, but I'm a jerk.

She gives a little laugh. I stop and press my face into her hair for a few seconds. When I pull back, we look at each other, both of us embarrassed and flustered. I lean forward to kiss her. It's the first kiss for both of us, and I'm not really sure what I'm doing other than mashing my lips against hers. When it ends, I decide I need to figure out how to be a better kisser because I want to do it again.

The next night, I sneak Mina into Dad's garage where he keeps his collectible cars. He never comes down here in the evenings, so it's a perfect place to be with Mina away from prying eyes. We're still dealing with the fallout from the other Knights. Nate and Eric took it well, but Kai ran off. I know Mina's worried about him, but there isn't much we can do.

Sitting on the floor, Mina lets me rest my head on her lap. We practiced kissing earlier, and I'm feeling rather smug. She's braiding strands of our hair together. I watch as she nimbly turns it into a ring. "There," she says with satisfaction. "A physical representation of this time." With solemn dignity, she hands me the hair ring. "A token of my favor."

I toy with the hair ring when a sound makes us freeze. I slide it into my pocket so I don't lose it as we wait. We hear voices followed by a giggle.

Two people enter the garage.

"Baron, you naughty man. You're late and you expect me to come at a moment's notice!"

Our eyes widen. That's Mina's mom.

"Euna, take your clothes off. We have to hurry before Eleanor gets back from the salon."

My dad.

I stand up holding Mina's hand tightly. "Dad?" My voice shakes at my father's betrayal. How could he do this to Mom again?

Mina's mother, in her underwear, gasps. My father has his hands on his belt. "Mina, Tristan, this is not what it looks like," Euna Steele says, her eyes going from me to Mina. "You can't tell your father, Mina."

"You can't tell your mother either, Tristan," my father adds. "It'll destroy everything. Divorces are messy, son. I promise you that this will never happen again. She'll get custody and take you far away if you tell your mother about Euna."

"Mina, if your father finds out, he'll divorce me," Mom cries. "You'll never see your friends again. Is that what you want? Please. Promise me you won't say anything."

I look at Mina. We don't want to be parted. I clench her hand and give a slight nod.

"I promise," Mina says, her eyes bright with tears as she looks at me. She's promising for us. For me.

My heart beats in gratitude. Mina feels the same way as I do. We can handle anything as long as we're together. "I promise, too."

We never talk about what we saw. Like a bad memory, we sweep it under a rug and focus on ourselves. We don't mention the incident to Kai, Nate, or Eric. It lingers as a secret that we guard.

In my desire to keep Mina with me, I never see the secret as a burden. It's another link that confirms Mina and I belong together. It's bad enough that Kai won't stop visiting Mina separately, or that Eric and Nate spend mornings with her without me. They're still trying even though Mina's picked me.

And maybe that's what bothers me more. If she picked me, why is she still devoting time to them? I want to be her everything. It doesn't help that Sean calls me a pussy for letting the others spend time with her. He makes the worst, most disgusting comments about Mina, speculating on what he thinks the guys are doing with her. He says she's too perfect and that she's hiding a kinky nature underneath it all. I shouldn't let Sean get under my skin, but sometimes, I think about his words too much. Sometimes, I feel doubt.

CHAPTER FIVE

Shin

THREE YEARS AGO...

I've been at Broadmoor Prep for a year. The fall will be interesting because Mina and I will be in the same school again. Broadmoor Prep's an interesting school if you like rich kids who have nothing else to do other than create drama. I've seen Mom watching *The Real Housewives of Beverly Hills*; like those women, it's clear that many students here don't have a grip on real-world problems. There's a bizarre hierarchy of elite students that give themselves a name every few years. I know that Tristan's already staked his claim. When he starts with his other Knights and Mina, they'll come in as the ruling group, taking over from the Aces.

Four guys fawning over my sister. If that doesn't spell trouble, I don't know what does. Mina's always drawn attention whether she wanted it or not. She's not your normal girl: a bit too mature, a bit too kind. I like the four boys well enough. Because I'm usually in charge when it comes to keeping Mina safe, her friends ultimately become my friends.

We moved here because Mom outspent Dad's last job. Dad's parents live close by, but they hate Mom and detest us because they firmly believe Dad married Mom because she was pregnant with me. I know all of this because I listened in on one of Dad's conversations with my grandparents. When I confronted Dad, he admitted it was true. Nonetheless, his parents agreed to help finance a "modest home" in this neighborhood with the possibility of welcoming their grandchildren if Mom learns to "behave." Dad's on a tight leash, which Mom resents.

When it comes to moms, Mina and I didn't get the worst, but Mom is far from the best. In a nutshell, Mom acts like Mina's a burden. In Mina's baby pictures, Dad's always holding Mina. Mom fawns over me at times, but as I get older and more aware of Mom's neglectful treatment of her only daughter, it taints our relationship.

Dad, on the other hand, is awesome as far as fathers go. He loves us. He dotes a bit more on Mina – she's a cute kid, after all. If he gives Mina a little extra affection, I don't mind because Mom is about as warm as an ice cube.

I've seen the boys change around Mina. From close friendship, to open admiration, and now... Let's just say that I'm worried that Mina will have to decide between her boyfriend and her friends.

Dad's been grilling me about Mina and Tristan. I get it. Tristan doesn't look at Mina with puppy eyes. There's something more. The kids in this area are hyper-sexualized at an early age. The girls flirt and act provocatively before they're fourteen. This is not about clothes. They literally come up to me and ask me if I want to fool around with them. I'm fifteen. I might be scanning a few magazines or surfing the net, but I'm not going to act on any thoughts right now. The boys here brag about things they really shouldn't be thinking about. Our old neighborhood was just a lot more grounded. Kids got to be kids longer.

Dad wants me to shadow Mina and Tristan. How gross is that? Do I really want to see some boy get all kissy with my baby sister? That's all they're doing, right? They're fourteen, after all. Okay, if I think about it too long, I know I'm going to get worried.

I start looking at the fall training schedule for basketball when Dad bursts into the kitchen with Mina in his arms. Mina's bawling. Mina never bawls. Her wails fill the air, and my skin gets cold and clammy hearing her cries.

That's when I notice that her dress is torn on the top, her lip is bleeding, and there are marks on her arms. Scratches. One looks like a bite mark. A human bite mark. I start shaking as Dad puts Mina down gently. Why does she have a bite mark on her skin?!

Dad rarely gets mad. Sometimes, he gets terse with Mom, but I've never seen him truly mad. Right now, Dad's face is red, and there are beads of sweat on his upper lip. He's breathing like he ran a marathon. His blue eyes barely recognize me as he starts rattling off instructions. "Shin, I need you to listen very carefully. Take your sister upstairs and help her clean up. Get her warm, okay?" When I nod, he grabs my shoulders. "Son, you need to be strong for Mina right now. That King boy, Sean. He grabbed your sister." Mina's wails grow louder when Dad says the name.

I might throw up. No, I want to go with Dad and beat Sean up. What the hell? "Did he ra—" I can't finish the word. "Dad! Did he?" My voice cracks. I'm getting hysterical.

Dad shakes his head, his breathing harsh and furious. "No, I heard her screaming. There was a girl there, too, recording this. I'm going over to the King household because Sean's going to pay for this. This can't be swept under a rug. There will be justice for Mina, you understand?"

Mina's fallen to the floor. I see the flash of her leg and hip. Why is her underwear missing? I can't move, but I have to. My sister needs me to keep it together. Dad crouches down to Mina. "Mina, my little girl, this isn't your fault. You didn't do anything wrong," Dad whispers. "I'm going to fix this. I promise you."

Then Dad is gone, murder in his eyes, leaving me uncertain.

I'm scared to touch her. What if it makes her sick? "Mina?" I try and say her name as gently as possible. I think. She's scared, and she's cold. I kneel beside her. I need to explain everything I'm doing so it doesn't alarm her. "Little bug, I'm going to touch you, okay? It's just me. It's just big brother Shin." I sound stupid, but that's not important.

Very slowly, I move. I gently grab her hand and her head snaps up, a feral snarl on her lips. I still. And then she blinks. She throws herself into my arms, sobbing. Her pain rips through me in a way I don't expect. How many times has Dad asked me to watch over her? How many times have I tried to protect her? Guilt seeps into me, and I want to cry, too. Why would anything do this to a girl? I know horrible things happen to people all the time, but it's supposed to happen to other people, not to my sister. I've never liked Sean. I thought he was a pig, but I never expected he would do this. Why Mina?

I scoop her up, relief filling me when she doesn't pull away. She seems so light in my arms, so insubstantial. Does she even know what's happening? Has she disappeared into her mind?

Mina stops crying. Her face becomes a blank canvas of tear stains as I settle her on a chair. My first thought is that I need to get her warm. In the bathroom, I fill her tub with warm water. Should I put in bath salts? I curse my stupidity.

When Mina's teeth begin chattering, I pick her up and lower her, fully clothed, into the water. I should probably help her undress, but I'm not sure if that's something she can handle right now. I locate the fluffiest and biggest towel I can find. I get her a change of clothes – something warm and comforting. I set them all on the chair.

She sits there in the water, her face empty and far away. She's lost in her mind right now. I run my fingers through my hair. I don't know what to do. "Bug, I'm going to wait outside, okay? But I'm going to come in and check on you every ten minutes. If you can, you might want to change your clothes. I put clean clothes here. The water will get cold and I don't want you to get cold."

I sit on her bed. Right now, I want a baseball bat and Sean's head. I wish I'd gone with Dad, but he's right that Mina needs to feel safe right now. If he finds Sean, I hope he hurts him. I hope he makes Sean pay. For a few minutes, I allow myself to cry.

Briefly, I toy with the notion of calling the guys. Tristan.

God. When he learns what Sean did to Mina, he might kill Sean himself. They're only fourteen, but those boys are a force to be reckoned with. My bigger worry is how this will impact Mina's ability to love and trust others. I hate the thought of Mina losing that big heart of hers, that ability to be compassionate with others.

After nearly ten minutes go by, I'm about to stand up when Mina comes out, hair wet but fully dressed in clean clothes. I take a closer look at her and notice that her lip is a little swollen. She comes and sits beside me, fat tears rolling down her cheeks. She's shaking again. I put my arm around her, grateful that she doesn't flinch.

"It'll be okay," I say, not knowing if what I say is true. Mina's strong. She's a fighter. It occurs to me that we may have washed evidence away. Wait, do I want that for her? A trial? Shit. I don't know. Sean's eighteen. He deserves to go to jail, but I don't know if that's what's best for Mina.

Her head falls heavily onto my shoulder. I do the only thing I can at that moment. I hold her and rock her until she falls asleep.

Minutes go by, or is it hours? I fantasize about a dozen different ways I could hurt Sean. I think of at least five ways I want him to die. I doze off and on, and then I wake suddenly.

After a while, nothing but continued silence greets me. Mina remains still and asleep beside me. Not wanting to bother her, I lie there trying to collect my thoughts. And that when I hear the sirens.

Dad must've called the police. I feel a sense of satisfaction. I want to see Sean get dragged across the lawn. I want to see his face knowing we won't let him get away with this.

I carefully move away. I can't tell if Mina's still asleep or if she has her eyes closed. "I'll be right back," I say softly. Maybe I shouldn't leave? When she doesn't respond, I decide to leave.

There's a strange flutter inside me, a sense that something has gone horribly wrong. The police surround the King manor and when I approach, the police stop me.

"You can't be here, son," the officer closest to me says.

"My father is in there," I say numbly. "What's going on?"

"There's been a shooting," the officer says.

I must've heard that wrong. A shooting? Did Sean shoot my father? What the hell happened? I try to push my way through, but the police won't let me.

That's when I see Eleanor King, screaming and crying. "She shot him! She just came and shot her husband and my husband!" Her eyes find mine. "Oh, God, your mother's gone insane, Shin! She killed your father!"

I stop moving. She has to be wrong. Dad's not dead. I need him. Mina needs him.

A paramedic tries to calm Eleanor down as I piece things together from Eleanor's continued screams and the police talking around me. Paramedics rush past me, jostling me, but I can't move. I hear the police report that the paramedics have declared two men dead. Mom's been arrested. I look around, trying to find a familiar face in the madness. That's when I see the four Knights, pale and horrified. My eyes meet Tristan's and there is a dark coldness in them. Something's gone wrong. I don't know what's going on, but I need to get back to Mina.

A police officer takes my name. She asks my age and asks about Mina. It hits me. If Dad's dead and Mom's being arrested, what happens to us? Will our grandparents come for us?

A hand grasps my arm. I look down and stare at my sister in her bare feet. Her mouth trembles as she takes in the scene before her. She hasn't seen the Knights. No, right now, she's too terrified to look around. If Dad's gone, Mina's now my sole responsibility. Whatever happens, she can't see me scared or out of control. I take a deep breath.

Sometimes, you don't ask to grow up. It just happens because life turns out that way.

CHAPTER SIX

LESS THAN THREE YEARS AGO...

Life can change swiftly and without warning. A few months ago, the most beautiful boy declares he loves me. I love him as much as any fourteen-year-old can. Then a monster grabs me. He tries to rape me. Even though I'm saved by Dad, I lose him the same day. He dies at my mother's hand. The boys, the ones who I thought were my Knights, my friends, never show up. I never hear from them. I'm not stupid. They have money. Their parents are powerful. They know where my mother is. The truth is that they aren't looking for me.

We are not sent to my grandparents. They don't want us. We're sent to my uncle in Texas at my mother's request. Mom never told us she had a brother: Uncle Soong. This chapter in my life is one that I want to forget, though. You see, this is when my life goes from bad to crazy.

When Shin and I meet my uncle, the first thing he tells me is that he's been reborn, and his new name is Uncle Michael – or more accurately, Archangel Michael.

In a surreal fashion, Shin and I become the latest members of God's Army. Here, the men have been hand-selected by our reborn Jesus to create the new members of the army. The way Shin presses my hand during our "education period" keeps me quiet.

It's a harsh orientation. I'm not properly obedient, but after the first few beatings, I become quieter. I don't want to break. I refuse to break.

After a few weeks of my insolence, I'm called before Jesus. I never learn his real name.

"Mina." Jesus smiles at me. "So sweet. So young. Truly. You are a blessing. A gift. Blessed will be the children you bear to join God's Army."

The men surround me. I'm in nothing but my shift. The horror of my situation makes me tremble. I don't want them to touch me.

Shin, toiling in the garden, stops. He looks at me in concern. I shake my head slightly.

"Mina, do you know why you have been brought to me?" Jesus asks.

I shake my head. I don't trust myself to speak.

"Your defiance. It comes from the devil, you know. He makes you want to fight me."

I flinch when he touches my face.

"You see, my touch frightens you because you know your sins," he intones. "I will properly bless you and cleanse you." He gestures to two men.

They grab my arms and hold me as Jesus approaches with a knife. Fear fills my face.

"Be not afraid, Mina. You will be healed." His words make my skin crawl.

Then I gasp as he cuts my clothes off me. Shame. Horror. I hear Shin scream, "Don't you touch her! Don't touch my sister!" He comes running.

My uncle and a guy who calls himself Archangel Gabriel grab him. They bring him towards us and pin my brother to the ground.

I force myself not to react, not to make it worse for Shin. A harsh stream of cold water is directed at me and in my face. I think I might drown, but I bear it. I can do this. I try not to scream and cry. When the lashes start, I'm too shocked to scream. When it stops, I see the leers. I'm shaking as Jesus wraps me in a burlap cloth, the rough material scratching my injured skin.

"Go back to the women's quarters and be healed of your sins," he intones.

I know they will hurt Shin. I see him on the ground and the rage on his face. When the switch is raised, I sob in earnest. I try to block out the sounds. I try not to feel. When I get back, one of the kinder women – Theresa – gently guides me to my room where she applies ointment to my marks. She doesn't speak. It's too dangerous to speak.

That night, Archangel Uriel takes a girl only two years older than me to his room. She's sobbing as she's dragged off. When she returns, she's shell-shocked and there is blood on her shift. The older women tend to her.

Parted from Shin, I break a little. I learn to be a good member of God's Army. I call my uncle Archangel Michael. I bow when Archangel Uriel continues to take the girl to his room regularly.

I'm too young for ceremonial coupling. Jesus declares girls must be sixteen. My memories of Tristan become harsh in my mind. Not all touches are innocent or wanted. I see the way the "archangels" look at me. It makes me sick.

Every day, I listen to their nonsense. I say the right things. Every day, a part of me shrivels. Maybe a part of me dies. I don't know. My solitude gives me time to think, and that time makes me realize that my Knights abandoned me the day I lost my father. Now, I only have Shin. I do my best to hold on for him.

I try not to think of Kai's protective warmth, Eric's friendly smile, Nate's easy banter. I especially try hard to forget gray eyes that made me think of storms and romance.

Sitting in the stifling warmth of my room, I only know that I'll die before I let them rape me when I turn sixteen. Sometimes, the only way to defy someone is to rob them of what he wants.

CHAPTER SEVEN

PRESENT DAY...

People often misuse the word karma. They think it means destiny or fate. It's a Buddhist (and Hindu) concept. It's the belief that a good deed leads to a beneficial effect, while a bad deed leads to a future bad effect. I don't believe in karma. I believe shit happens and sometimes we're destined to have a shitty life.

I am not a "woe is me" type of girl. I've had good days and a whole string of bad days. There's no point in weeping over the injustices of my life. Some people have had it far worse.

As Shin and I arrive at my grandparents' manor, I try not to shiver. Shin's been my official "guardian" for nearly two years. It's not as strange as it sounds. After God's Army, nothing is strange anymore.

Three months ago, we learned my paternal grandmother, Evelyn Steele, died. After Dad died, my paternal grandparents never contacted us. They never came to find us. If they had wanted us, they could have fought for custody. Anything would have been preferable than dead Uncle Soong. I wonder if Greg Steele gave us a moment's thought before he died. Imagine our surprise – my surprise, really – when we learn that Grandmother Steele has left everything to me. Not to Shin. Just to me. But there's a stipulation to the will. I must live in Steele Manor and graduate from Broadmoor Prep Academy. Until then, the money is controlled officially by the estate – a.k.a. lawyers.

"It's just one year," I say to myself. Finish senior year and

I'm done. As we stare at this strange home, I tell Shin, "It doesn't feel like home to me. Nothing really does, I guess."

It's a lonely life Shin and I lead. We have each other and no one else. Everyone else either abandoned us, betrayed us, or ignored us.

Shin hugs my shoulders. He has become surrogate mother, father, as well as brother. "As long as we're together, right, little bug?"

Shin should be in college. Instead, he spends his days worrying about me. I'm his burden. When he escaped God's Army one night, I thought he died. Life lost all meaning in the two months I mourned him. After the raid – when we were finally reunited – I've tried to piece myself back together. It hasn't gone well, but Shin started working as soon as he could. Ironically, we inherited Uncle Soong's meager estate. It wasn't a lot, but with both of us working while e-learning, we didn't need much.

"You're too good to me," I say.

Shin laughs, trying to chase the shadows from my face. "You're my favorite sister, Mina."

It's an old joke. "I'm your only sister," I mumble back.

As we walk to the house where my father was born and raised, the door opens. The butler's name is Alfred. I try not to laugh.

"Mrs. Allen is waiting for you in the main living room, Miss." He's very formal even though he isn't wearing a traditional butler outfit.

Mrs. Allen has been running Evelyn Steele's household since her demise. Now that we're here, Shin and I won't make any changes unless Shin deems it necessary. He's the better judge of character. I've stopped caring about people. It's too hard.

Our fears are allayed. Mrs. Allen – her first name is Marie – is soft and efficient. She immediately offers me some tea and has all the information we requested at the ready. "You two must be exhausted," she says with a sigh.

Shin and I are private. We don't ask her what she knows

about us and our past. We don't ask what rumors swirled about us during our absence. I take the tea and walk to the window, staring at the gardens that remind me of my life years ago – those brief years when I was truly happy. Shin immediately goes through legal and business matters. He has a better head for it, to be honest. I sign where told. I find the real world too exhausting.

Unwillingly, my thoughts drift. Tristan. Kai. Nate. Eric. Are they still here? Do they hate me? If I see them, what will they say? What will I say? So many questions, so few answers. If they ignore me, I'll be fine. I'm always fine. I embrace the numbness and emptiness. I like it. I know Shin's looking for therapists in this area, but I'm tired of talking. I'll play along. I'll go to appointments to keep Shin happy. He's all I care about now.

"Mrs. Steele had a hard time accepting your father's death," Mrs. Allen says, and I turn at her words. "Of course, when she heard about your uncle –"

Shin cuts her off. "We don't talk about that very much. I understand what you're trying to say." He glances at my very pale face. "Maybe we should pick our bedrooms? Won't that be fun, little bug?" He uses my childhood nickname with affection.

I nod, putting down my cup.

After dinner, Mrs. Allen checks in with us. "I'm sorry about earlier. I didn't mean to pry or say anything offensive," she says. Her demeanor is soothing, guileless.

Shin mutters some reassuring words, but I interrupt him. "Why did Evelyn Steele leave everything to me? Do you know?"

Mrs. Allen's forehead puckers. "Because you were your father's favorite."

My breath catches. A flash of pain. Daddy. Shin covers my hand. I want to ask why she never looked for us. But what's done is done. That past is simply that.

"Your grandparents were proud. Too proud. I think that's why their son moved away," Mrs. Allen says quietly. "They could never admit a mistake. I think in death, this is Evelyn's way of apologizing." She bids us goodnight.

Shin tries to push some dessert at me. "You need to eat more," he insists, noting that I only picked at dinner.

I smile weakly. "Shouldn't I eat something more nutritious than cake?" I retort. I sit back and nestle into the plush chair. "Two weeks until school begins."

Two weeks until I face the world again. It's easy to hide, to live in a cave. I'll have to face people. I might face *them.*

"I think it'll be good to get out. I'm only a phone call away if something happens while you're at school," Shin continues in a reassuring voice. "You don't have to do this, though. You know I don't care about the money."

I look at my brother carefully. He's had to grow up so fast. I try not to feel twinges of guilt, but the guilt comes anyway. "You can't protect me forever, Shin. I'll be okay," I insist. I can do this for him.

Shin smiles. "Mina, you're strong. You're brave. It's one year. I'm already looking at possible colleges we can attend."

When he talks about the future, I want to cry. His optimism – does he fake it? When I shatter, on days when I break, he never does. I won't do that to him again. He's suffered enough because of me. I look out into the darkness to compose myself. "I'll cramp your love life," I respond. "No one will want you if your kid sister hangs around."

Shin huffs. "Then that person is not for me. We're a package deal, Mina. I won't abandon you."

The night clouds shadow the moon. "I know, Shin. I know."

Later that night, in my room, I pace the confines. This is what I did back in Texas when I wasn't permitted to go outside. Sometimes I would dream about when I was happy, but I stopped doing that when it only made me despair more.

As I child, I remember reading about Pandora's box. According to Greek mythology, all the evils were unleashed due to a woman's curiosity. The only thing that remained was Hope. Without it, mankind would have been doomed.

Which means that one cannot live without hope. It's a grim thought, but one that resonates with me. The end of this journey doesn't come with a prize or even an acknowledgment. I know what it is like to lose hope. You can cling to the emptiness and despair or embrace the possibility of silence. Very few people truly deserve a terrible life. The rest that get one anyway? We're simply unlucky.

CHAPTER EIGHT

I rush to Tristan's place not knowing how I feel about the information I carry. This town breeds excess, and Tristan is the epitome of excess. Since turning sixteen, after rotating through several high-end sports cars, his next move was to move out of the main house. He now lives in the pool house, which is really a two-bedroom "apartment" situated on the other side of the enclosed pool. During summers, the pool opens up and is in constant use by us and those we invite. When the Knights throw parties, we inevitably end up here, watching girls vie for our attention. His mom could hardly care less about our shenanigans.

When I arrive, there is plenty of skin to be seen among the ladies – some are topless and trying to get our attention. Kai salutes me with a beer. Midsummer Sun, in a yellow bikini, is flirting with him outrageously. He tries not to yawn when I gesture him over.

"What's up?" he asks, stretching his neck. Midsummer is attractive in a deadly dull way. She'd get further with Kai if she kept her mouth shut.

"Guess who's back in town and will be attending Broadmoor?" Question for a question.

Brown eyes quizzical, he shrugs. "Beats me. Who?"

I can't tell if I'm filled with excitement, rage, or fear. "We need to find Eric and Tristan. They'll want to hear this," I say instead, pulling him behind me. When I get to the pool house, Kimberly Moore storms out, clutching her swimsuit to her chest. Her smeared lipstick tells me all I need to know.

"You're an asshole, Tristan!" she screams, tears streaming down her face. She's not hurt, but I can tell she's angry and humiliated.

"That didn't stop you from entertaining me," Tristan says in a bored tone from inside. "I must say, I may not want a repeat. That was sub-par at best."

Kimberly screams a list of profanities at him before running away.

I enter his place as he puts his trunks back on in the living room. "Dude, did you screw Kimberly Moore?" I make a face. Kimberly is a Class-A bitch and pain in the ass. I wouldn't touch her with a yardstick because she'd be the kind of girl that would get ideas from a one-night stand. This behavior from Tristan, though, shouldn't surprise me. Tristan's been going after girls since he turned sixteen, and not in the *looking for love* sort of way. Girls salivate over his money, unfortunately.

Tristan shrugs. "No. But that doesn't mean I can't use her in other ways."

Kai makes a sound of distaste. Kai's more selective when it comes to girls, but girls learn quickly that relationships with any of the Knights are dysfunctional at best.

Eric comes downstairs, laughing and shaking his head. Eric's less callous than Tristan, but he feels little pity for Kimberly. "Kimberly still can't figure out how to get you to sleep with her, huh?"

"She's boring. Good for occasional relief, but I don't plan to screw her," Tristan snorts. His gray eyes narrow. "What's going on, Nate? Either you've met a hot chick or something's wrong."

"Mina Steele is back," I say, watching their reactions. Kai curses, Eric closes his eyes, but Tristan goes completely still. So many emotions cross his face. From a distance, he seems calm and collected, but if you look in his eyes, you know it's a façade.

"I thought her grandparents disowned them," Eric says, opening his green eyes. "I know Evelyn Steele died, but didn't the money go to charity?"

Tristan is the volatile one, so we're watching him carefully. I shake my head. "Apparently, Evelyn Steele asked the executors of her will to find her grandkids. She left *everything* to Mina according to Father."

Tristan exhales slowly, a muscle twitching in his jaw as he begins to pace. "Guess Evelyn got soft in her final year of life." For a moment, he looks at his hands as if he's surprised that they're clenched. "Is she joining us as a senior at Broadmoor?"

"Yeah," I confirm. My father's connected at the school, so information on students is easy to come by. "Her tuition is paid. You know the school. They'd never turn down Steele money."

We're silent. We all have different memories of Mina, but the way things ended is a bitter one. I once thought the world revolved around her. Kai adored her. Eric worshipped her. But Tristan loved her.

"Where's Shin?" Kai asks, his voice gruff with emotion. His dark eyes are lost in the past. Does he still remember the long-legged girl who climbed trees? The girl who filled our loneliness with a pervasive presence?

"The staff at the manor prepared the home for two new residents, so he's probably with her," I guess, "but I don't know for sure."

Tristan's nose flares slightly. "Always getting whatever she wants," he mutters to himself. "Always getting away with everything. That bitch. She toyed with all of us. She toyed with *me*. She lied to me. To all of us." He lifts his gray eyes. That cruel streak we know all too well gleams in his eyes. "This isn't a curse. It's a blessing. I have a chance to make her pay for my father's death. We rule Broadmoor. Let's show our former queen that we no longer bow to her. I'll crush her before she can fool anyone else."

Kai's shoulders stiffen a little. He shifts from one foot to another. "We were kids back then, Tristan. Euna Steele pulled the trigger, not Mina. Why not just ignore her? Wouldn't that be payment enough? We can show her she means nothing to us."

This does not settle Tristan down. "My father's dead because of her!" Tristan shouts, getting to his feet. He crosses over to Kai. "Her actions led to the shooting. She broke her promise! And we can't forget about what she did with Sean." He glares at me when I open my mouth. "I know, she was only fourteen," he mocks me. "She knew what she was doing. Sean's a creep, but she goaded him on."

I bite my tongue and look away.

Kai nods slowly, his shoulders slumping. "What's your plan?"

After a moment, a harsh smile settles on Tristan's face. He snaps his fingers. "I got it. We'll loop the girls in. Maybe even give Kimberly free rein."

Eric exchanges a glance with me in concern. Kimberly's vicious. It would be more appropriate to keep this amongst ourselves. "Kimberly's hated Mina since they were in middle school," Eric says uneasily. "You know what she did to her when Mina started at the Lower School. Shouldn't we handle this ourselves?"

"Some of you don't have the stomach to do what's needed. This way, our hands stay relatively clean. Mina will remember Kimberly. It will be the icing on the cake." Tristan's face is cold. "I'll tell Kimberly she can have me for the school year if she can break our little queen. I'll just use earplugs when I screw her." He slides a glance at Kai. "Kai, you work on Midsummer. She's equal to Kimberly in every way. I'll bet if you give her the same incentive..."

Kai clenches his teeth in distaste. Great, we're now whoring ourselves out to get back at Mina? This is messed up!

But then I remember that Tristan's anger burns hotter than ours. His love for her was intense for a nearly fifteen-year-old kid. Honestly, I don't think he's really gotten over her. As Knights, we owe it to him to stick together; we need to back him. We're the Knights, which means we do things together.

Eric straightens. "No. You're right. Mina ripped us apart." He nods, albeit reluctantly.

Kai steadies himself after his initial surprise regarding

Midsummer. "She didn't just hurt you. She hurt all of us. And then she left us to pick up the pieces. She never tried to contact us or anything."

"I'm in," I say. I hope Mina is ready for the storm we're about to unleash. It isn't going to be pleasant. I hope I can stomach it.

Kimberly and Midsummer listen with too much glee. You'd think that after multiple brushoffs, Kimberly would be done with Tristan, but she's been lusting after him for far too long.

"Seriously?" She sways her hips as she walks over to Tristan. I'm sure she thinks she's sexy. "Oh, babe, this is going to be so much fun."

"Does she have to leave?" Midsummer asks. "Like, how do we know when we win?" She flicks coquettish looks towards Kai.

"I want her to cry," Tristan says, "in front of everyone. Break her or make her leave. Either is fine. Or do both." He smiles. "I wouldn't mind both." He leans in provocatively.

Kimberly's eyes flicker as she licks her lips. "Oh, I'm going to enjoy collecting my reward. I've wanted to punish that bitch since I met her. She was such a prissy creature, and she thought she was better than me."

Tristan may be smiling, but his expression is cold. "I'm all yours once it's done. And Kai's game if you help, Midsummer."

The two girls hook their pinkies together. I can't help but think we've made a deal with the devil.

CHAPTER NINE

Mrs. Allen says I'm free to buy a new car, but this BMW is barely two years old. It seems like a waste to simply replace it. Mom would want a new car. I am not my mother.

In my navy uniform, I look like any other girl going to a private school, except that I don't care about the school or what I look like. I know enough about Broadmoor Prep. My hair is not in a fashionable do, and I'm not wearing a smidgen of makeup. For that alone, I am not any other girl. If only people could see my thoughts...

"What are you doing today?" I ask Shin while eating a banana.

He frowns at my meager breakfast. "Well, we should get doctors and dentists set up. And I'm talking to several therapists to see if one might be a good fit for you," Shin says. He's so motivated.

I avoid talk of therapists. "Pizza for dinner?" I ask.

Shin notes the shadows beneath my eyes. "You are doing okay, right? Maybe we need an emergency session...." He trails off when I frown, my brow furrowing.

"No. I'm fine. Just nervous. Stop fussing, I have my anxiety meds. I'll be fine." My smile is forced and bright.

"For Christmas, we can do something fun," Shin suggests. "Go to Canada. I hear Banff is beautiful."

For Christmas? I don't even snowboard or ski. I try to swallow my fruit. "That'd be great." I'm trying. I'm really trying.

"I'll look into it," Shin says with a nod, satisfied with my pseudo-enthusiasm.

The drive to school takes under thirty minutes. When I arrive at Broadmoor Prep Academy, I stare at the students piling into the lot. My car isn't super flashy, but I don't stick out like a sore thumb. I recognize the posh girls, the fashionable bags and shoes, the little touches to the uniforms that indicate the wealth and privilege we have. Empty. Meaningless. Material goods can be washed away in an instant. If I can remain invisible, this experience will be barely tolerable.

Grabbing my bag, I head to the main building, eyes on the ground. No need to look at anyone. I'm not looking for friends. If I had an invisibility cloak, I'd use it. I'm barely across the courtyard when someone crashes into my back so hard that I face plant.

Delighted laughter erupts behind me. The voices clack around me. Young Mina might have wept. She might have bitten her lip and wondered who was being careless or cruel. Nearly eighteen-year-old Mina mechanically straightens her skirt and stands. It's been several years since I saw them last, but I would recognize them anywhere.

Tristan King is no longer a boy. Not quite a man but nearly there. He's tall, chiseled, broad, and beautiful. His fine black hair still has that faint wave, his gray eyes are still dark and stormy. There's an attractive brunette clinging to his arm, and it takes me a few more seconds to remember her. Kimberly Moore. She attacked me in the girls' locker room on the first day of school in seventh grade. She hated me because Tristan wouldn't give her the time of day. He doesn't seem to mind her now. I wonder if they're together. I wait for a slash of pain, but there is none. I only feel the hollow beat of my heart.

Next to Tristan is Kai Reeves. He's broader than Tristan – I wonder which sport he still plays – but they're the same height. His brown eyes hold me in contempt. It's odd seeing that emotion in his eyes. He'd been my protector, my champion. I don't recognize the Chinese girl on his arm as she obscenely rubs herself against him. (I'm not exaggerating. She has his arm between her breasts. What would Archangel Michael say?)

Eric Mansfield, my green-eyed Aquaman, no longer looks at me like I'm an angel. No, he smirks at Tristan like he's in on a private joke at my expense. Does he still sketch? Does the wind whisper inspiration to him? When our eyes meet, his slide away.

Nate Remington, my blond and devastating Galahad, is indifferent and impassive. I don't see his sensitive soul anymore, just a hardness that seems alien on him. He is not the Nate I remember.

I still remember driving away in the police car with their eyes boring into me in rage. My Knights who never came. They are not my Knights anymore. If I didn't know it before, I know it now. They are strangers wearing the skins – vaguely familiar but not the same.

I didn't expect them to be happy to see me, so I am not disappointed by their behavior. In many ways, I'm glad that we won't be friends. I won't have questions to evade or dark secrets to spill. My time here will be brief, and, in a snap, I'll be gone. I will fade and become insubstantial.

"What do we have here?" Kimberly coos, leaving Tristan's side. "If it isn't little Mina Steele." She slams her hands into me hard and I stumble back. "Where have you been? Slumming like Mommy? What's it like to have a parent in jail? Do you sneak in contraband for Mommy Dearest? I can't believe we have a convict's kid at our prestigious school." The girl on Kai's arm nods in agreement.

I don't lash back. I look at her evenly. "Hello, Kimberly," I say quietly. "Tristan. Nate. Eric. Kai." Saying their names aloud makes this moment real. I suppose deep inside that girl waiting for her Knights to save her wants to live again. I wish that girl would simply die and stay dead. I suck in my breath and force my mind to still. During my time with my uncle, I became adept at disappearing from the world.

"You don't talk to us," Tristan says in clipped tones. "You don't look at us. We rule this school, and you're nothing but a trespasser. You were never one of us to begin with. You don't belong here. You're trash. Everyone will treat you as such." He grabs my wrist and hauls me forward. "Your time here is going to be miserable, Mina. And when you cry, I'm going to be the one smiling."

I stare at him. I don't see a trace of the Tristan I knew – the boy who wanted my heart at fourteen. "I'm sorry about your father, Tristan," I say. I can't help it. It's something I've wanted to say to him for years.

Tristan's eyes darken in rage. "Don't you fucking talk to me!" he snarls, his hand gripping so tightly that it's certain to leave a mark. He looks like he might even hit me.

I wait, eyes lowered, for the strike. But all he does is throw me at Kimberly, who uses my hair to yank me off balance.

"Let's go. There's nothing to see here," Tristan orders. I guess Tristan's still the presumptive leader.

Kimberly twists my hair painfully before kicking me in the shin. I gasp in pain. As they walk away, I see Nate glance at me furtively. But I don't cry. No. If I could cry, it would mean I still understood emotional pain.

Sometimes I wonder why I bother doing schoolwork. I suppose I like the mindlessness of it. After I left – that is, after my father died and my mother went to jail – I first went to school online, and then I was homeschooled, and then I was sent back to school online. Because my academic credentials are spotty, Broadmoor had me take several exams to decide where to place me. Fortunately, like Shin, I'm academically talented. At night, textbooks were friends. Sometimes they were the only friends I had.

As Mr. Kim begins his class on differential equations, I flip through the material. The class will be relatively simple as I read up on the topic two weeks ago. The Chinese girl I saw earlier is Midsummer Sun. She's in my math class as is Nate and Tristan. As requested, I don't look at them or acknowledge them. But apparently, it isn't enough. Midsummer trips me and my ribs smack into the edge of a desk.

"Miss Steele, do be careful," Mr. Kim says in alarm as I stifle a sound.

"Do be careful," Midsummer mocks softly as I press a hand to my ribs with a faint hiss.

I glance up briefly at her and see that Nate and Tristan don't look thrilled. I guess they thought I'd be in tears now. Or perhaps they hoped for a more severe injury. *Sorry to disappoint you, boys. Bruises are nothing.* I straighten my skirt and head silently to my next class.

By the time lunch rolls around, I've been tripped and pushed more times than I bother to count. A bruise forms where Kimberly kicked me. My skin over my ribs purples unattractively. The Knights make it clear that I will not be protected. When I enter the lunchroom, everyone goes silent. I know something is about to happen. It's Kimberly who throws the first roll. The other students follow. Near Kimberly, at a round table, Tristan, Kai, Nate, and Eric watch me coldly. They don't throw rolls. No. They just want me to know it's on their orders that I'm being pelted.

I turn around and leave. I don't run as a few more pieces of bread are launched at me. I'm not hungry anyway. Outside, I breathe in the clean air. It'll be cold soon enough. I imagine the numbing cold as I dig my fingers inside my sleeve and pinch the skin of my forearm hard. The sharp pain gives me a sense of relief. Physical pain. Pain tells you that you're still alive. Emotional pain just means you're vulnerable. I rub at the scab on my shoulder. Some of the tension leaves me. I've got this. I can do this for Shin.

Oh, Tristan. If only you knew that your words don't scare me. Maybe what you need to use is a physical weapon. Not even you can hurt me now.

CHAPTER TEN

Even when Mina was our queen, I thought her delicate. She bruised easily even though she climbed as many trees as we did. Fearless but sensitive, if we got hurt, she'd run over to see what she could do. When one of us had a bad day, she'd sit quietly until things got better. She'd leave us tiny gifts: a pretty rock, a pressed flower, a fortune from a fortune cookie.

Those memories make it hard to accept what she did, but Tristan saw the proof. Of us all, he has the biggest gripe. Not only did she deceive us, but she spilled a secret that caused the death of Tristan's father. Mina lost her dad, too, but she brought it on herself.

For two weeks, Kimberly and Midsummer have been relentless. They have extra help from Sarah Yeats and Karen Markle. The girls corner her in the restrooms, pushing Mina around. They call her a murderer's daughter. They taunt her about her horrible mother: a mother who couldn't spare time for her daughter. Mina becomes the victim of our ability to hate. She has soda thrown at her while people call her names. People push her in the halls. She doesn't react. She doesn't cry. She doesn't beg for mercy. She doesn't fight back. It's like she's not even there. The blankness in her face is scary at times.

Nate is antsy. "I don't like this, Kai. I mean, at what point do we become monsters? We're being shitheads and assholes. Yes, Mina hurt us, but there isn't an hour that goes by when someone isn't doing something to her."

Eric sips his drink as we watch Mina enter the lunchroom. She never stays long because Kimberly inevitably does something or starts something. In the past two weeks, I haven't seen her eat a single thing. Now that I look at her closely, she's gaunt. She's always been slender, but now she looks bony. I can see the sharpness of her elbows through the stiff uniform. The waist of her skirt looks loose. She walks quickly to grab some chocolate milk before leaving, but Kimberly still manages to pelt her with a fork.

The girls around Tristan laugh heartily, but even I see the way Tristan's eyes narrow briefly. Either he doesn't like that Kimberly threw a fork or he realizes that Mina's far too thin. He may claim to hate her, but there's more than just anger in his gaze.

Midsummer saunters up to me in a way I don't like. "Kai, baby, we have something special planned for that annoying girl later this week. Make sure you're in the parking lot when we tell you to be there." She runs her fingers up my arm. "I can't wait to see you at the swim meet this weekend. Do you want me to come over after to help you celebrate when you win?" She does this annoying flutter of her lashes while she licks her lips. My skin crawls.

"I'm good, Midsummer." I can't believe I agreed to date her if she and Kimberly get Mina to leave the school or break down completely. It's going to suck when Mina does fall apart.

Nate lowers his head. "What are you girls doing?"

Midsummer pouts. "Don't ruin our surprise, Nate. Let's just say I can't wait to claim my reward."

I rub my neck. "I'm going for a walk. I need to stretch out a bit."

When Midsummer tries to come with me, I shout, "Alone! I need to walk alone."

Once I'm outside, I breathe a little easier. There's a nice breeze and I'm surprised more students aren't out here. I see something move among the trees along the path that goes around the school. I know who it is. Don't ask me why I start following – I just do.

I find Mina staring blankly out in the field. She doesn't hear me approach, but I swear I think I hear her talking, whispering. I can't make out the words. Her left arm is limp, and her right hand seems to be inside her jacket like she's putting something away. Is she crying? If she's crying now, does this mean Kimberly and Midsummer have won? I catch fragments.

"...bad... punish... suffer the... sins..." She doesn't sound like she's crying, but her shoulders are shaking a little.

I hate that I want to check on her. Tristan says I'm too soft. He's not wrong. A part of me wants to ask her if she needs something. I take a step and wince when my foot lands on a branch.

Her shoulders stiffen. She puts something away in her pocket before turning slowly. She's not crying. Her face is completely devoid of emotion. I'm not even sure she recognizes me. She blinks twice. "Kai." She says my name like she's trying to remember who I am. She returns to her perusal of the field before her.

"You knew we'd be here and still you came back," I say finally, bitterness making me harsh. "It wasn't enough to destroy the friendship between us."

"You all blame me... for that?" She sounds puzzled.

"That and more. You know what I'm talking about," I snap. "You could have had any one of us and we would've been fine with it. Instead, you had to dirty yourself. I guess it's our fault for putting you on a pedestal. You're nothing but a whore to us now."

The word shocks her. Mina gasps, her forehead wrinkling just a little. "What did you say?"

"A whore. Tramp. Slut." I let each hateful word fly off my tongue. I grab her by her arms hard. "Do you like that?"

When she takes too long to respond, I kiss her hard, my hand holding her head still. For a second, she's in shock. Then she twists, fighting me like a she-demon, her hand connecting with my cheek with a resounding crack. Her nails cut my face as she pushes free.

I feel like a pig when she stares at me in horror. She trembles as her mouth snaps shut. "I see," she says. I hear a hint of pain – the first real emotion from her – before that impassive wall returns. "Don't touch me. Don't ever touch me again."

Her words confuse me. What confuses me more is the way her lips move silently – I'm not even sure if she's aware that I'm still here. Her breathing is uneven. As I look at the way her shoulders shudder, I notice a dark mark on her left shoulder. "Did you spill your milk on your jacket?" I ask suddenly, overwhelmed by my actions and needing something mundane to focus on.

She blinks, looking down. She sucks in her breath. Again, no tears. Her eyes flash at me before she runs off. It's then that I notice that her chocolate milk is on the ground, completely unopened.

When I return to the guys, no one asks me about the marks on my face.

A few days later, Tristan follows Mina from Literature class. He texts me to join him in the hallway. The students part when they see us stalking her. I'm still shaken from my encounter with her, so it's Tristan who drags her into the girls' restroom. "Get out of here, now!" he barks at the girls staring at him in shock. Once they leave, he locks the door.

Mina stares at him numbly. "What do you want, Tristan?"

"I want you to leave," he snarls at her. "I'll be nice. I'll give you two weeks to taste what life is like without the entire school after you."

There's a strange exhaustion on her face. "I can't leave. My inheritance is based on graduating from Broadmoor, Tristan."

"Don't say my name!" He paces in front of her. "Fuck!

I should've known it was about money. You're just like your mom. She was a greedy little bitch!"

Mina averts her head. She won't look at either of us.

"You must like pain," he continues erratically. "Why else would you be here? You're twisted like your mother." He stops. "I have to know. Why? Why did you do it?"

Mina glances at me briefly. "Do what?"

"Everything!" he roars. A muscle twitches in his jaw as he shakes her. I hear her teeth snap shut. "Why did you break our secret? My father would be alive today if it weren't for you."

When he stops shaking her, Mina's brows come together in confusion. "What are you talking about? I—I didn't."

"Don't lie to me!" Suddenly, the anger fades. "Don't lie to me. At least, have the decency to be honest about what you did," he repeats, his eyes bright. "Why? Why Sean?" he asks.

"Sean?" Horror flickers over her face, cutting through that façade.

Her expression bothers me. Is she upset that we know? Or is it something else? "We know what you did with Sean," I say, and whatever color she had in her face disappears.

"I know about Sean," Tristan says coldly. "You know how I felt about you. And you let him touch you just because you were jealous."

"How could you know about Sean?" she asks, her eyes huge in her face. She looks sick.

Tristan shakes his head. "He told me, Mina. He had a picture."

She sways. "You saw a picture? There was... a picture?" For a moment, she shakes visibly in front of us. "And you – you're not upset with Sean?" Her hand presses into her left shoulder, her nails digging into the jacket.

Tristan pulls back with a sneer. "He had the decency to confess to me!"

"Decency?" She flinches. "He... told you." Her voice is a bare whisper.

"I would've done anything for you back then. I spent the

past few years trying to forget you. You mean nothing to me now." Tristan eyes her with disgust. "I've replaced you over and over again, Mina, and discarded you just as fast."

She covers her mouth with her free hand as if to stifle a sound.

"I'll give you two weeks to get the hell out of here. Then I'll send everything at you, Mina. I won't stop until you're nothing but a shell." He leans forward. "I won't stop until I make you bleed over and over. I want you to suffer."

She blinks at us while we leave.

All four Knights are waiting in the parking lot as Kimberly and Midsummer requested. "Tristan," I say, "maybe we should ask the girls to let up on Mina."

Nate's eyes widen hopefully, but Tristan frowns at me. "Getting soft again, Kai? After today, she gets two weeks. That's my offer."

I'm about to defend myself – and possibly Mina – when she shows up. Her head is bent – she never looks up – and her silky black hair covers her face like a curtain. That's when I see Kimberly and Midsummer run at her, slamming into her back as hard as possible.

Mina's body goes flying over the asphalt, her hands breaking her fall. Even from where I am, I can see that she's bleeding from her knees and hands. She doesn't scream or cry out. How can she handle the pain? The way she moves, she's clearly hurt. That's when I see the scissors. I'm taken back to seventh grade.

With glee, Kimberly reaches for a lock of hair and starts hacking away. I can't stop the protective surge that overwhelms me to stop Kimberly. It's not just me – we all move at the same time towards Mina.

But someone beats us to her. Pascal Takeda is there, grabbing Kimberly's wrists, wrestling the scissors away, and flinging them to the ground in disgust. He's on the swim team with Eric, quiet and unassuming. "What are you two doing? Leave her alone, for God's sake!" he shouts, rattling Kimberly with a little shake before pushing her away. "She's not even fighting back! What's wrong with you?!"

We're there a second later. I take a moment to evaluate Pascal. He's not a small guy. He's got a swimmer's physique: upper body strength, little body fat. I've not seen him in a fight, but if he fights like Eric, he's not one to be taken lightly.

"Kimberly, Midsummer!" Tristan barks with barely contained rage, his gray eyes hard. Any illusion of composure is gone – he's visibly shaken.

Mina remains on the ground, eyes downcast, parts of her hair hacked off at her shoulder. There's something devastating about the way she doesn't fight back. Her bloody hands leave marks on her books as she picks them up. For some reason, I think about all the gravel and rocks that must be embedded in her wounds.

"I get it, you're the Knights and what you say goes," Pascal snarls at us, and it's the first real anger I've ever seen from him. "But for God's sake, grow up! Look at her!"

Eric blanches at Pascal's tirade as if Pascal's struck a nerve.

"You know nothing, Takeda," Tristan snaps right back at him, his eyes growing wild when Pascal reaches for Mina. "Don't you fucking touch her!" To everyone else, Tristan sounds like he wants her to suffer, but we know his words stem from jealousy.

Nate and Eric are there, holding Tristan back from landing a blow. The last thing we need is Tristan to beat up one of our best swimmers. Kimberly and Midsummer watch with annoyance, but Kimberly's eyes are fixed on Tristan. At least they've backed off. I'll hit them if they do anything else. We never authorized them to brutalize Mina like this!

Completely ignoring Tristan, Pascal puts a hand on Mina's shoulder, and she flinches violently. "Don't!" she shrieks.

Her teeth flash as she snarls. I don't expect that.

Her reaction doesn't faze Pascal. Instead, he bends down on one knee, holding his hand out where she can see it. "I'm not going to hurt you, Mina. Do you need a hand up?"

I've never felt shittier in my entire life. I've assaulted her and now let two girls brutalize her. We've sunk to a new low. As I watch Mina stare wildly at Pascal, us, and the girls, it's like a knife in my gut.

Tristan abruptly makes a grab for Mina, as if he can't bear the thought of Pascal touching her but freezes when her bloody hands fly out in panic. "Don't touch me. Don't you touch me," she blurts, cringing, horror crossing her face when she realizes her words. This isn't humiliation and emotional pain. Her face mirrors terror and confusion as she takes in her surroundings. She sees Pascal's hand, and she forces herself to accept the help. And then Pascal is lifting her, helping her with what she's dropped.

She's a mess. Blood runs from her knees, and her hands leave streaks of red when she tries to straighten her clothes. She must be in pain. She's shaking, but it's not in anger. Her eyes grow distant and the shaking fades.

"Thank you," she says, and there's a flash of gentle Mina before she disappears. "I'll be alright. I'm fine." She wobbles her way to her car, never looking back.

We watch her drive off silently.

CHAPTER ELEVEN

The weekend starts painfully. Shin doesn't believe I fell in the parking lot. I don't know how to explain my hair either. "Mina, what happened to your hair?" he asks me. "Who's doing this? Does Tristan know? Nate? Are they helping you?"

"We're not friends anymore," I say wearily. "I told you that. They blame me for what Mom did."

"Did you cut your hair?" Shin asks very quietly, his brown eyes worried.

I'm silent.

"I should talk to them," Shin says, rubbing his neck. "I'm sure they wondered where we went."

No, they didn't. We're not worthy of them anymore. "No!"

"Mina, for God's sake—"

"There *is* no God!" In many ways, I hope I'm right because I'm damned if there is one. Maybe I'm damned either way. I walk to the window. "Stop. I don't want you to do anything. The guys aren't doing anything." Lie. "I'm fine." Lie. "I have it under control." Lie.

"Mina, I'm technically your guardian—"

"Don't you dare throw that at me." I glare at him so hard that he raises his hands. "You can't protect me from the world, Shin. My hair's a wreck because I was trying to prove a point." Lie. Lie.

His voice gentles. "Alright. Okay. I am not controlling you. You know that. I... won't get involved. It's killing me to see you like this. You can trust me."

Shin knows. He knows that he can't control me. He knows that setting too many rules or interfering too much is detrimental to my mental health. It's because of me that he struggles. It's my fault Dad is dead. It's my fault that Tristan lost his father. It's my fault that Shin doesn't have a life, that he had to save me over and over. The guilt gnaws at me until I want to scream.

"Bug, let me help you. Please."

"It's fine. I'm fine." Lie. Lie.

Shin growls. "You're not fine. You're wasting away. You look like shit!"

I flinch.

Shin grimaces. "I'm sorry, Mina. I didn't mean to yell. Let's just leave. We don't need the money. We can move away from the memories here, get a fresh start somewhere else."

I'm a bad sister. A terrible sister. "I'm really tired, Shin. I'm going to go to bed early."

"You haven't had dinner," Shin says. "Take a shower. I'll bring something up, okay?"

I draw myself a bath, running it as hot as I can stand. While the tub fills, I take scissors and chop off the odd lengths of hair. My eyes narrow as the hot water touches my skin. I only wish it were hotter. I hiss as the water touches my cuts and scrapes. The pain clears my mind of dark thoughts briefly. With a washcloth, I go to the fresh cut on my shoulder. My skin heals remarkably well, and I don't cut too deeply. Still, if Kai had looked closer the other day, he might have noticed it was blood on my uniform. I need to be careful. The blood on my hands and knees melt into the hot water.

There's a knock on my bathroom door. "I've left some soup and bread for you on the table." Shin is quiet for a second. "Mina, promise me you'll eat it."

My poor brother. He sounds ready to cry. "I will, Shin. I promise." No lies this time. I can do this for him.

When I know I'm alone, I take a moment to think about Tristan. He knew about Sean. He blamed me. I still remember

Sean whispering in my ear. *You think Tristan will want you after I'm done with you, little girl? Nope. He'll blame you. You'll be ruined.*

I sit in the tub until the water cools and my fingers wrinkle. I wipe myself carefully then apply ointment to my knees and hands. Then I check the cut on my shoulder right by my armpit. I slather on ointment before putting on a big Band-Aid. There's not much to do about my hands and knees.

In a soft fluffy robe, I eat my cold soup slowly. I don't taste it. I just shovel it down my throat before starting on the bread. As I promised Shin, I eat it all.

There's a strange irony in having had my hair hacked at by Kimberly twice in a lifetime. To please Shin, I get it professionally trimmed. I have a lot of hair and it was getting too long anyway. It doesn't bother me.

When I return to school, Pascal Takeda is there waiting for me in the parking lot. He's an imposing figure – tall, well-built, strong. He glowers at students around us as he walks purposefully to my car.

Pascal becomes my new protector. I don't want his help, but he intends to meet me every morning and walk me back to my car every afternoon. When I tell him it's not necessary, he simply shrugs and continues to be there when possible. He's not a Knight, but he's prominent enough that he's capable of fending off Kimberly and her goons.

Sad but true, I don't remember Pascal. My social circle was small in middle school, and my Knights – I mean, the four boys – made it challenging for anyone to befriend me. But he remembers me.

"You protected Kimberly when the Knights punished her for trying to hurt you the first time," he recalls. "It made an impression."

Pascal brings me lunch from the cafeteria. I don't deserve his kindness. When I say so, he looks at me. "Why? You haven't done anything terrible."

"Bad things happen to people because of me," I admit. There. I've admitted it. I didn't deserve what happened to me, but because of me, others have suffered. I pick at the sandwich.

Pascal thoughtfully regards me. "The Knights were happy around you. They lit up when you entered a room. I won't ask for further details, but you had no control over your mother's actions. You didn't put the gun in her hand. I don't see how Tristan can blame you for that."

Tristan blames me because of Sean. This is something I refuse to discuss with Pascal. Does Tristan think I tempted him? If I did, haven't I been punished enough? I check myself. No, there is no balance to suffering. There is no karma. There is no rhyme and reason. I consider myself lucky. My terrors are mostly psychological, not physical. That makes me somewhat fortunate, right?

"Takeda!"

I jump when the Knights show up at our little table in the hallway. Tristan's lips thin when he sees me with a sandwich in my hand. Is he angry that I'm eating? Maybe he will only be happy when I'm dead.

Pascal leans back with arrogant ease. "What?"

"I thought I told you that no one gets to help her," Tristan says in a dark voice. "I'd hate to turn the school against you, too."

Pascal glances at me and then at the Knights. "Would you? I'm the second-best swimmer on the team. There's a good chance Eric and I will take top honors at state. I don't know why Mina doesn't go to the principal about you guys, and I'm not going to harass her about it, but I'm more than happy to take my talents elsewhere. I'm sure the admin would love to hear why I want to leave. I'm sure the papers will ask why I suddenly left Broadmoor."

"Tristan." Eric's voice is full of warning.

Tristan's jaw clenches. I never thought Tristan and I would become enemies. Then again, I never thought I'd be dragged into a cult. It's laughable. I drop my sandwich back on the paper and wrap it up. Without speaking, I stand up, dusting the nonexistent crumbs off my lap. I barely took a bite, and this morning's breakfast was a granola bar. I find lately that food is not essential.

"Mina, you haven't eaten," Pascal says.

"It's okay. I'm fine." Lie. "I had a huge breakfast." Lie.

Pascal slams his hand on the table. "Is this necessary, Tristan? Look at her! She doesn't have any weight to lose! At least let me try to get some fucking food in her!"

Kai flinches. Nate turns away. Eric is unhappy. Tristan's eyes go wildly from me to Pascal. "Why aren't you eating?" Tristan asks as if I have the answers to everything.

The truth is that I don't get hungry. Food is a tether. Why would Tristan care anyway? "I eat." Lie.

"She doesn't eat because no one leaves her alone long enough to eat!" Pascal's exasperation shows.

Kai crosses his large arms. "We'll leave you alone for lunch." The four look at each other and agree.

"Mina," Nate begins, but then he shakes his head as if I'm not worthy of his thoughts.

Kai and Nate were always the two softies. It almost makes me smile until I remember Kai grabbing me. I don't want their pity. It's better for them to hate me fully anyway. "Don't," I say gently. "Don't. It won't change anything."

Tristan looks startled. "What do you mean?"

My smile is almost sad. It's fitting that I'm back with them in this weird, disjointed way. I wish I could wipe the anger and resentment from their faces, but that's beyond my power now. The first time I saw them together, I wanted to care for them. Nothing gave me greater pleasure than seeing them smile. Nothing gives me pleasure now.

"Nothing," I say. "I mean nothing."

I don't look back when I leave.

CHAPTER TWELVE

Something about my pallor or behavior causes Nate to seek me out later in the week. I have a free period after lunch and Nate takes it upon himself to hunt me down.

"Are you sick?" Nate peers down at me.

When I shake my head, he blocks me from leaving. I back up warily and sit back down. I have to look up at him anyway. I should, at least, do it comfortably.

"Mina, we just want you to leave Broadmoor," Nate says. "You have all this money. You can go anywhere."

This again. I sigh. "It's not that simple. I told you. My inheritance is contingent on graduating from Broadmoor. Shin wants to go to medical school, and I want to help him achieve that goal."

"I'll pay for it," Nate blurts. "I'll pay for Shin's medical school. You can leave and I'll give you the money."

Briefly – just briefly – my eyes widen in surprise. Oh, Nate, I would've accepted your help at fourteen. But not now. There were nights in Texas where I begged the unforgiving sky to tell them I needed them. What would Nate say if I told him I cried to sleep begging for Tristan? Then, when hope faded, I cried for all of them. In my pathetic naivete, I believed that they would eventually look for me. Now I know better. Except for Shin, bonds of friendship and love are fleeting and easily broken.

"I don't want your help," I tell Nate. "I'm doing this alone. I will never rely on you four ever again. Money will never buy me."

Nate jerks back as if I slapped him. "You never wrote." Nate's blue eyes shimmer. "Did you ever think about us? Did you think about Tristan? All these years... You never wrote. You just left."

I laugh without humor. "Did you ever look for me?" I counter. When he doesn't respond, my lips twist. Of course not. They assumed everything. "I didn't think so. By the time I could, it was already too late. What does it matter now? You four have already judged me."

"Tristan won't stop until he's hurt you," Nate blurts, and I wonder if he's worried for me.

I try not to laugh again because it would sound horrible and broken. Something ugly and angry unfurls in my chest as my memories invade me. "You can't hurt me, Nate. Tristan can't either. Not in the way you think. And if you don't have the courage to tell Tristan that, I will tell him myself."

This time when I stand up, Nate lets me leave.

True to Tristan's words, there is a reprieve in attacks on me. I suppose the Knights think when it restarts, I'll start crying. That's what they don't understand. I don't cry anymore. Yes, there are bad moments when I'm weak. Yes, sometimes I don't have the energy to stand up. My tears dried up long before I came back.

I tell Pascal I need to do some work in the library after school. Instead, I make my way to the pool. I know Eric comes here to practice every other day, and it isn't unusual for the other three to wait for him.

When I get there, I'm glad that it isn't crowded. I had planned to talk to Eric first, but when I see the other Knights chatting, I change my mind. The order doesn't matter.

As I approach them, Tristan's mouth tightens. At least Kimberly and Midsummer aren't here.

"I'm not leaving," I say quietly. "I don't need your pity and a two-week reprieve."

Kai crosses his arms. "You know what will happen." He and Tristan exchange a glance.

"I do." I face Tristan. "Tell me, Tristan, what will placate you?" Before he can speak, I say, "Do you need to hit me? Do it." I step towards him as he stands up, his eyes wide. "Need a weapon? A knife? A belt? A whip? A switch? Go ahead." I spread my arms wide. "Come on, Tristan, what are you waiting for?"

"What the fuck, Mina," Tristan swears, looking nervous for once.

"I'm right here," I taunt him. "I won't fight back. You want me to suffer, right? So, do it!" My hand curls around the box cutter.

Tristan recoils before he sneers. "That would be too easy. I want you to suffer."

"Suffer? Why not just kill me?" I hold the box cutter out. "Here. I'm waiting. Or are you too scared? Can't do it yourself?" I smile. "How about I ask Kimberly? Don't give me a two-week reprieve. I'm tired, Tristan."

"What's wrong with you? You act like you want to die!" Nate snaps.

My smile disappears. I should want their hate, their anger. It makes my choices easier. Then why am I here? I'm mocking them. I glance at Kai. "If that's the only way you know how to function, then so be it. But if you're expecting tears, think again. It would require a heart to break." I take another step forward, noting the way Tristan steps back. "But don't send Kimberly to do your dirty work. That's just pathetic. Have the guts to take me out yourself."

The copy of Evelyn Steele's will flutters from my fingers. Of course. I suppose Shin felt he had to lie.

I suppose it's better this way. Shin can have his illusions. And I can move forward with little guilt. I stare at my reflection in the mirror and bring the sharp blade to my shoulder. *Just a little cut.*

CHAPTER THIRTEEN

Nate

When Mina was troubled, I was the one she turned to. Mina's relationship with her mom was tenuous at best. Before the betrayal, I used to wonder why Mina ended up with such an awful mother. It was hard watching her mother's indifference. I worried about her as children. I find myself worrying about her now.

Mina's not eating.

Mina's too thin.

Mina's... not well. That's what my gut tells me.

After her rant towards us by the pool, we've been watching her. In math class, Tristan and I glance at Mina periodically. Midsummer snickers at Mina after calling her a monster. I force myself to remain stoic, but something in me screams that this needs to stop.

Thanks to Pascal Takeda, Mina's being harassed less. I want to hate the guy, but a part of me is secretly grateful. *By the time I could, it was already too late.* The way she said it. The way she confronted us bothers me. She's no longer the expressive, sensitive Mina. New Mina is a shadow: she has Mina's shape and voice, but she lacks emotion.

"Miss Steele, are you paying attention?" Mr. Kim asks Mina suddenly.

Mina blinks and looks at the notes on his board. "Yes," she replies, her tone perfectly flat.

"And what am I talking about?"

Midsummer sneers, but Mina doesn't miss a beat. "You're using the chain rule to explain implicit differentiation."

Mr. Kim is surprised but pleased. Midsummer stops cackling. Mina returns to her still repose. Not once does Mina acknowledge that Tristan and I exist. It… bothers me. Except for confronting us at the pool, she doesn't acknowledge anyone. In the halls, she walks like a zombie, going from place to place mechanically.

I need to talk to the guys.

When it comes to Pascal Takeda, Tristan is torn between annoyance, anger, and jealousy. After helping Mina in the lot – to be honest, we were about to go postal on Kimberly – Pascal injects himself into Mina's life. She doesn't seek him out, so we can't blame her. No, Pascal does it all on his own.

"We're still within the two-week reprieve I gave her," Tristan insists, but I know he's worried. He can lie all he wants, but Mina is getting under his skin. He sees that she's unwell. He freaked when she offered him the box cutter. Why was she carrying a box cutter?

"Tristan, why can't I go after her now?" Kimberly pouts.

Everything about Kimberly throws me off. She's so keen on hurting Mina. Why Tristan is using her to go after Mina is beyond me. She's repulsive.

"You weren't supposed to physically touch her!" I shout.

Kimberly ignores me, sitting on Tristan's lap coquettishly. With a snarl of disgust, he throws her off. "You asshole!" she screams. "What is your damn problem?"

"You don't get me until after Mina is dealt with," he hisses. "I *told* you to harass her, not hurt her!" Tristan grabs Kimberly fiercely and shakes her viciously. "You touch her like that again and I'll break every fucking bone in your finger!"

"You said to break her!"

"We didn't mean physically!" I shout. But honestly, that doesn't make it any better. Everything we're doing fills me with unhappiness.

Midsummer – what a damn annoying name – puts her hand on her hips. "Why should we listen to you? You're just limiting us." She licks her lips as Kai enters the room. "Maybe we'll just move forward without your say-so."

"You cross me and I'll destroy both of you!" Tristan shouts, pointing at them. "Get out of here, Kimberly. And take your bitch friend with you."

After a slew of insults, Kimberly leaves with Midsummer. Tristan treats her horribly – not that she's a nice person to begin with – but why Kimberly keeps coming back is beyond me.

"You need to calm down," Eric says. Tristan turns on him with fire in his eyes. "You're not fooling us, Tristan. You still want Mina." He looks at Kai. "You do, too."

I stop Tristan from going after Kai, shaking my head. "Look, man, if you still want her – if either of you still wants her – you need to think about how far this is going to go. Because once you cross a certain line, there's no going back. Mina's not going to forgive you."

Kai's eyes widen. Recently, an air of guilt surrounds Kai every time he sees Mina. Has he crossed a line with Mina? I remember the marks on his face all too well. I can't imagine Kai doing anything too forward. We know he had strong feelings for Mina once. But he backed off years ago. What if he doesn't want to back off anymore?

"Don't you dare," Tristan says through gritted teeth. "After everything she did to us. To me."

"I'm not the one obsessing about her constantly," Kai says quietly. "She was fourteen when everything happened. She made a mistake."

This is not the first time we've mentioned this. The facts: Mina was under the age of consent and Sean was legally an adult. There are laws about touching a minor. Now that I'm eighteen, the narrative is even more nauseating.

"Whether it was consensual is irrelevant," I decide to say. "Sean was in the wrong touching a fourteen-year-old."

"It doesn't excuse what she did to my family." Even to my ears, I sense Tristan wavering.

No one responds. Tristan's complaint sounds childish and petty. We're eighteen and holding a grudge against a girl who was fourteen when the events happened. It sounds... pathetic. Whether we want to admit or not, a part of us wants Mina to stay.

"What do we do now?" Eric asks. "Because once the two weeks are up, Kimberly's going after Mina again. Is that what we want?"

Tristan's mouth flattens. "I need to think."

Yeah, we all do. I just hope Tristan comes to a decision sooner rather than later.

CHAPTER FOURTEEN

Mina

As part of our senior year activities, the school sends us on a whale-watching trip. The thought of being trapped on a boat with a bunch of classmates is not appealing. Again, Pascal's appointed himself my protector. The Knights almost seem jealous of Pascal's attention, but considering how they dislike me, I'm probably wrong. Maybe they're just mad that someone is defying them.

On the shuttle ride to the harbor, Midsummer sits on Kai's lap, laughing and ruffling his hair. The school's permitted us to be out of uniform, but Kimberly's skimpy top doesn't seem appropriate for the possibly wet and cold boat ride. At least she has a puffer jacket. She spends a great deal of time walking up and down the aisles, swaying her hips and bending provocatively. Tristan seems to flirt back, but when she runs her hand down his chest, he pushes her away.

"She really shouldn't throw herself at him that way," Pascal remarks. "It smacks of desperation."

"He seems to be okay with it," I say drily.

Pascal purses his lips. "I don't know."

On the boat, we're shown where the life jackets are before we sail out. Pascal grabs me a hot chocolate, and I find myself enjoying the trip for a bit. When I go to the restroom, my cheeks are pink from the wind. I have a half-smile on my face.

Before I can return to Pascal, I'm stopped by Kimberly and Midsummer. "Are you throwing yourself at Pascal now?" Kimberly asks. "The things you'll do for attention."

Isn't that ironic? I doubt Kimberly would understand. Midsummer says, "Your dumb innocent act doesn't work at Broadmoor. We know what a whore you are. I can't believe you threw yourself at Sean. We saw the pic. It wasn't enough to have the Knights drooling all over you, was it?"

I stumble. What did she just say? My shock must show because Kimberly starts to laugh. "Aww, you thought we didn't know about how you let Sean touch you? How you begged him?"

I can't speak. Did Tristan tell them? Why? Even if he blamed me, I was fourteen. "If you don't leave, we'll tell the whole school. I imagine several guys are willing to test out how willing you are and how you like it rough. Isn't that what Sean did to you?" Midsummer sneers. "Imagine how much fun that will be."

What they say doesn't cause fear; it causes nausea. *Don't feel. Don't think.* I walk away. I don't think I can breathe. There's a shout that someone sees a whale. As students crowd to one side, I head in the opposite direction. I can't be near anyone. The boat has slowed to idle speed, and I stand astern alone, the rocking of the boat taunting me. My hands grab the railing. Breathe. I need to breathe.

Never forget you are unclean. Only I can make you pure. When the children of archangels grow in your womb, you will be truly blessed.

I clench my hands to my ears. I can't make the voices stop. I hit my head with my hands. I need to feel a sharp pain to bring me peace. Anything to stop the voices.

He'll blame you.

I suppose I did tell Tristan he couldn't hurt me. I was mostly right. I just didn't think he'd expose my shame to the world. This must be his hate shining through. I suppose the blame falls on me. I expected something physical from him, not emotional. This is too... visceral.

"Mina?"

I can't have people know about Sean. It makes me too

vulnerable. The memories dredge up a mix of guilt and revulsion. It's too much. Dad died because I couldn't stop Sean. I was too weak. I'm still weak.

I throw up over the side of the boat, but I don't feel better. I can't stop the intrusive thoughts. My despair forms before me, and like a black hole, it swallows every part of me. Tristan couldn't do the harm himself, so he sent Kimberly. He couldn't break me physically, so he... I should be angry, but I'm not.

"Mina?"

A hand grabs me. I scream. "Don't touch me! Don't!" My hands fly up. I attack like an animal, caught between the past and present. "Get away from me!"

"Jesus! Mina! Stop!"

"No!" I shriek, breaking free. I don't think. I climb over the railing because I need to escape. I didn't escape last time and it led to calamity.

"Mina, what are you doing? Come down!"

I jump.

I don't remember the fall, just the sharp slap of the water. It breaks me from the past and brings me to the bitter present. It's cold, dark, and disorienting. I'm battered by the waves, thrown under. I want the cold. I want the pain. I want the silence. Distantly, I hear shouts. I think I hear my name.

I've never been a great swimmer. My body spasms in the water, fighting for air, but I force my body to embrace the cold, embrace the water. The waves push me under, and the roar of the water is painful and glorious. A memory of Kai leading me around the pool flashes in my mind. I remember Tristan staying in the shallows with me. I recall Eric and Nate putting me on a raft so I could play in the deep with them. Laughter. Sunlight.

I feel a hand, a yank. Suddenly, an arm grips me around

the waist, and I'm propelled to the surface. My lungs involuntarily spasm as my mouth automatically seeks the air. My lungs hurt as it forces the water out. I cough, struggling to free myself.

"Mina, I can't hold you up if you fight me!" The words come out like a plea. Tristan?

That can't be right. The waves hit my face. I gasp, craning my neck, as the arm tightens around me and I feel the warmth against my cheek. Gray eyes meet mine, wide with fear…for me. "Let me go, Tristan." I don't know if he can hear me. I push at his arm on my waist. "Let me go. Please."

"No, keep your head above the water. I have you. I have you." His lips are right by my ear, panting. He's trying to get us closer to the boat, but he's tiring. "I'm not letting you go." His voice is hoarse.

Somehow, I manage to shout, "Let me go! You'll die, too!" I try to loosen his grip.

I hear more sounds and shouts. My bleary eyes become aware of Eric and Pascal heading towards us with a bright orange life ring buoy.

"Don't give up, damn you. Not on me." He doesn't shout, but his lips are so close that I hear him. "You're not leaving me. Don't you dare." He's trying to move us closer to Eric, but he's fighting the waves and the currents and me. "Please, Mina."

If Tristan doesn't let go, we'll both go under. The waves buffet us, and I sputter, trying to clear my face. I don't care about me, but I don't want Tristan's life in the balance. Depression is selfish, but I'm not so far gone that I'll take another life with me. I let fate decide, passively waiting to see if we'll tire before Eric and Pascal reach us.

Fate works against me. Eric relieves Tristan briefly, shoving me onto the buoy. I'm too tired to fight, the cold weighing my limbs as Pascal rearranges my body. I slump uselessly as Tristan uses his body to hold me against the floatation device. The three work as a team to move us back towards the boat. I don't know how they can move. I feel so cold.

We're pulled in by the ship's crew. Tristan and Eric force

me out first. I collapse on the deck, Nate barely catching me as I cough uncontrollably, my lungs burning. Kai places a thick blanket over me, lifting me in his arms and carrying me inside.

I'm dimly aware of Tristan, Pascal, and Eric being placed near me. Kai and Nate guard us against curious students as the teachers chaperoning the trip start making phone calls. Tristan struggles to move, but he manages to make his way to my side. Cold, long fingers clasp my face as he looks at me with haunted gray eyes.

"What the hell, Mina," he croaks at me.

"You should've let me die," I tell him sadly, ignoring his shock.

I close my eyes and shut down.

CHAPTER FIFTEEN

In science, we're taught that the right answers are found only when we ask the right questions. I find myself with a lot of questions but few answers. So, I'm either not asking the right questions (likely) or I already have the answers (unlikely).

My mind replays Mina's actions. I don't know what convinced me to check in on her. Maybe it was the pallor of her face that I could see even from a distance. Maybe it was the sheer despair that echoes at times within me. As soon as I moved her way, the other Knights followed. When she pressed her hands to her ears, when she didn't recognize any of us, all my anger and resentment disappeared. My gut churned because I could see the horror in her face. But touching her triggered a reaction I never expected.

You should've let me die. Her words echo over and over in my head. She jumped to escape me. She jumped to escape all of us. She wanted to die. Acknowledging that hurts like real physical pain.

Concerning my actions, I didn't think – I had to get to Mina's side. Thank God Eric and Pascal had the sense to grab the buoy. In that instant, I knew fear, but it wasn't for myself. It was the fear of facing life without her. When I reached her, even as she fought me and told me to let her go, even as my body struggled to keep her head above water, I knew that either she would survive, or we would both go down. Trying to survive without her was not an option.

When we get back to port, there are ambulances. Mina's

in a bad way – hardly responsive and pale. How long was she in the water? How much water did she swallow? Her shadowed eyes indicate she hasn't slept well. The paramedics insist on taking her to the hospital, but when I try to join her, I'm refused. It's tempting to throw a tantrum. I'm a King – I'm rarely denied anything. I'm a few seconds away from forcing myself inside Mina's ambulance when Eric asks to go to the hospital, too. He pretends to be shaken and dazed. We're thrown in the second ambulance.

On the way there, I know Eric's thoughts echo mine. We did this, didn't we? I did this. Some twisted part of me thought seeing her suffer would alleviate the childish grief I've held on to. It didn't. Instead, it threw us into turmoil. I know in my heart that Mina was never to blame. Mina didn't pull the trigger that killed my father. As children, we were asked to keep a secret – in essence, lie to one parent to protect the other. How was that even reasonable to begin with? Then with Sean... He's my brother, but I don't like him – I never have. I'm not willing to think about him just yet.

Mina's spark – that bit of joy she brought to us – is missing. Mina's mimicking the motions of life, and I've been blind. She's perilously close to falling off a ledge, and all we've been doing is pushing her closer.

Once I'm checked out and cleared, I'm given dry scrubs to dress in. Since I'm eighteen, I can technically be released on my cognizance. It takes me a bit to convince a nurse where Mina is, but when I tell the nurse I'm Mina's boyfriend, she gives me the details.

The curtains are drawn, but I stop when I hear the doctor say, "Your sister has suspicious injuries on her arm."

"I saw them. I think she's cutting herself."

I haven't seen or heard Shin in years, but I recognize the voice. It's a shade deeper and rougher than before, and he sounds defeated.

"The injuries do appear self-inflicted. Considering the report that she jumped on her own, we'd like to keep her here under observation for a psych eval," the doctor continues. "As she's technically a minor, I need to report this to CPS, of course."

What the hell? I force myself not to barge in as a heaviness settles in my stomach. Self-inflicted?

"I know. I wasn't aware she was cutting herself. I have her in therapy. I don't know what else to do."

"She should be hospitalized."

"No! You don't understand. It's been tried, and it made things worse. Another round would kill her. I can't lock her up after all she's been through."

Mina's cutting herself. For a moment, I can't breathe or think straight. The box cutter. She has a damn box cutter! Does she hurt herself at school? She's hurting herself and all we did was yell at her.

Mina's always been the grounded one, the one we leaned on. And now... What have I done? I could have lost her today. The mere thought of anyone locking her up... No. No one is locking her up. If I need to use every favor, I will. No one will take her away from me.

And that's the crux of it. I need her. My heart beats for Mina Steele. My heart knew it before my mind did. Eric and Nate saw through my bull quickly. They saw how quickly my world began to revolve around her. I should have kissed her the moment I saw her again. Instead, I may have irrevocably harmed the one person who matters to me.

After Dad's death, Mom had the house torn down and rebuilt before she sold it. At my request, we moved, purchasing a lot where we could custom-build. With Sean heading to college, the design and layout were left to me and Mom. The main part of the home is smaller, but in keeping up with the neighbors, we've added amenities. The house is designed to entertain. My mother throws lavish parties, inviting numerous Broadmoor Prep families. On the premises, we have an in-ground, indoor pool attached to a solarium on one side and the pool house on the other. When I turned sixteen, I moved into the pool house – really a two-bedroom, self-contained, home. I loved my father and love my mother, but we were never one of those families that did everything together. My mother's love for me is kind but distant. Not much has changed since Dad's death.

The Knights assemble at my place, and to say that we're gutted is an understatement. The trauma of the day's events affects us differently. For Nate, he sits before the fire in dark contemplation. He likely blames himself for not speaking up. Eric swims – I would think he'd be tired of water – but he'll swim to the brink of exhaustion before talking to us. Kai takes one look at me and swings. I welcome the pain. We lash out because we don't know how to deal with the pain and turmoil in any other way. We're not trying to kill each other or hurt each other. But we need the distraction to still our minds.

When Eric climbs out of the pool, his chest heaving, he doesn't hide the tears that mix with the water streaming down his face. He leaves the pool area, a towel barely absorbing the water, and slumps in the middle of the living room. For a while, no one speaks to me. Of course, they blame me. I started the vendetta, and now I have no defense. I'd feel better if they took turns kicking me in the gut.

Nate speaks first. "How do we fix this? I mean, with what she's doing to herself, we don't want that to continue. We want to help her." The passive plea that states what we all want – fix, forge, rebuild the connection with Mina.

But it's Eric who voices my niggling fear. "What reason did we have to believe Sean over Mina anyway? And what is happening to Mina? What's eating her up so much?"

I close my eyes. Sean wouldn't have lied, would he? Yet, I must consider that Sean willingly crossed a legal boundary with no remorse. That means Sean is a monster. But if Sean is a monster, what does that make me?

Would Mina even trust us with the truth?

"Sean is irrelevant right now," I finally say. I stop, remembering the way my heart pounded as I held Mina's body in the water, and how desperate I was to save her. "I was wrong to blame her. We were wrong. We need to undo the damage."

Kai nods heavily as Nate claps him on the shoulder.

"But can we undo what we've done?" I ask.

The other Knights have no answer for me.

CHAPTER SIXTEEN

All weekend, my mind replays Mina jumping off the boat. She didn't fight the waves, she didn't even try to swim. Tristan's face mirrored mine – shock, terror, pain. When he jumped, I knew he'd get to her. It bought me time for my training as a lifeguard to kick in. Mina's never been a strong swimmer. Tristan's sole thought was to reach her; my sole thought was to ensure I could save her life.

She wants to die. That thought crossed my mind more than once swimming towards her. I'm a hell of a swimmer. So is Pascal. We're aware of how the cold can hamper your endurance. And we weren't dressed properly. Our clothes weighed us down. Through sheer focus and discipline, Pascal and I reached them. The look on Tristan's face as he tried to keep Mina's head above the water...

With the threat of a possible lawsuit – can you imagine the headlines: "School doesn't enforce lifejackets on boat!" – the school gives Mina a week to recover at home. When I find myself looking for her at school, I know I'm not the only one. How many times did we pretend we weren't scouring the hallways for her? Scanning the lot, looking for her BMW, looking for her bent head. She tried to be invisible, yet we always saw her. With all that's happened, I'm willing to forgive and forget. I only hope Mina will, too.

Guilt is a powerful motivator. With Mina recuperating, we start making changes right away. The first is putting Kimberly and friends in their rightful place. We start by declaring

Mina off-limits.

"Listen up!" Tristan says loudly during lunch. "Mina Steele is not to be harmed. She is under our protection. If anyone hurts her, touches her, or breathes on her the wrong way, you will answer to us."

Kai walks around the room, rolling his shoulders. "Does anyone have a problem with this?"

As one, the students shake their heads. Kimberly and Midsummer frown at us.

"When Mina comes into the lunchroom, you will treat her respectfully," I state. "You let her sit where she wants to sit." The truth is that I want Mina to sit with us. In my opinion, it's where she belongs, but I'm not going to announce that.

Nate positions himself next to Tristan as Kai continues to prowl the edges. "If I catch any of you speaking negatively to Mina – if you even speak negatively about her – you will answer to us. You will not harass her, period." Nate directs his words over to a furious Kimberly.

Kimberly stands, her petulant face growing sourer by the second. "Where is this coming from? You said we should crush her? Or is she screwing one of you now?" Kimberly hisses. "You wanted her gone!"

Tristan's face freezes – people tend to think Kai is the brute. Tristan? He's the truly ruthless one. He walks over to Kimberly. "What did you say?"

A hush falls over the room at Tristan's quiet question. Kimberly's trying to defy him, and we need to crush that quickly. Kai cracks his knuckles to signify that being female won't protect her. I doubt he'd hit her, but then again, it's Kimberly. Karen, Sarah, and Midsummer edge away from their ringleader. So much for solidarity. I smirk, watching Karen cringe. When Kimberly opens her mouth, Tristan leans over and whispers something in her ear. She pales.

"I am going to ask you again, what did you say?" Tristan repeats the question icily.

"Nothing. I didn't say anything," Kimberly whispers,

lowering her eyes.

"Good." He continues to glare at her for a bit before dismissing her.

As we sit down to eat, Nate says to me, "Phase One complete."

We show up at Steele Manor a few days later. On our drive there, I come to terms with my feelings. Pretending to hate her was easier than missing her. Despite that, in the middle of the night, there were times I thought about her, wondered about her.

When Mina and Tristan started dating, I was angry and jealous. We all were. That's what made us so pathetically susceptible. By making her the villain, it justified my resentment.

We'll never recapture those few years of our childhood: that open trust, that open comfort that changed the moment Tristan pursued Mina on his own. But I'm not sure we'll survive if Mina doesn't forgive us. I never stopped loving Mina, but my feelings have evolved. I'll be what she needs, whether it be a lover, a friend, or a brother.

The Steele Manor is an imposing structure in this neighborhood. I can't imagine Mina being happy here because the manor lacks personality. Mina loves homes with character. She loves turrets and hiding spots and cozy rooms. Steele Manor is just… huge.

We're taken aback when Mrs. Allen greets us but refuses us entry. Tristan is not having it. That arrogant King personality flares into life.

"I'll call the police!" the woman threatens.

Tristan squares his shoulders, glancing at me. "Do it. Between my family and Eric's, the police would be stupid to interfere."

He barges his way in, the rest of us following. The four of us go from room to room, calling Mina's name, until Shin runs out to intercept us.

Shin used to be a lanky guy. In the past few years, he's gotten huge. His dark eyes sweep us in disgust. "Get out of here!" he barks. Kai sizes him up, ready for a fight. Kai is broader, but there's a swiftness to Shin's body we don't miss.

"Not until we talk to Mina," Tristan says in a hard, cold voice.

Shin and Tristan stare each other down. "No, not now." Shin stretches his neck. "You guys have done enough."

"We saved her life!" Tristan shouts.

Shin laughs. "You are a piece of work. Tell me, what was going on at school? The cuts, the bruises, her hair. You were letting people bully her, weren't you? The great Tristan King. Did it make you feel like *a man*? Did you do anything to help her?"

"It's complicated," I try to explain, "but we're here to make peace."

Shin snorts in disbelief. "Peace? For what? Are you at war?"

Mrs. Allen comes in, her face flushed. "I tried to stop them," she says.

"Thank you, Mrs. Allen," Shin says. "I have this."

We get a resentful glare from Mrs. Allen before she leaves. Tristan waits until we're alone.

"I'm not leaving until I see her," Tristan says, lifting his chin arrogantly.

A broken sound escapes Shin's lips. He ponders us for a minute. "You want to see what you've done? Will it make you feel better? Will it bring you *peace*?" He mocks us. "Fine. Follow me."

He walks off, heading down a long hallway until we reach a room that is devoid of all furniture. Inside, Mina walks around numbly, her eyes on the floor.

"Mina." Her brother says her name with exhaustion.

Mina continues to pace slowly, ignoring us, ignoring her

brother. She looks tiny and frail in an oversized sweater and sweats. When Shin approaches her, she freezes, her hand going to her left shoulder. She starts to claw at her shoulder.

"Stop, bug. Stop." Shin's voice is gentle, tender, as he tries to capture her hand.

Her head snaps up and a feral snarl escapes her lips. "Don't touch me!" She spins, her nails digging in deep.

Tristan moves, grabbing her hand. "Mina, don't!"

She shrieks, twisting away. Tristan drops his hand, his eyes wide and confused.

"Are you guys happy now?" Shin asks bitterly.

Mina backs away, her eyes still on the ground, until she's against a wall. Her breath is uneven.

I clear my throat. "Mina, we're here to talk." I remember how Pascal approached her that time in the parking lot.

Walking slowly, I keep my hands down. When I'm sure she can see me peripherally, I show my hands so she knows I won't touch her. "Mina, it's Eric. We're not angry, sweetheart."

For a while, Mina does not react. Her eyes dart around until she raises them to stare at me. Her face goes from confusion to anger to passive disinterest. "Get out."

Nate shakes his head. "No, Mina, we're not leaving you, not like this."

"Get out." Her lips tighten.

"You jumped deliberately," I say loudly, and everyone in the room freezes at my declaration. Tact has never been a forte of mine.

I hear her harsh breathing. Maybe it wasn't the right thing to say, but she is reacting. That has to be better than that mindless pacing. Just as I think that she starts pacing again, but her movements are focused and slightly manic.

She stops in front of Tristan and narrows her eyes. "Why did you save me?"

Tristan stares at her with pain in his eyes. "I wasn't going to let you die." His voice is rough with emotion.

Her nails dig into her shoulder again. The pinch of her

eyes tells me she's hurting herself. She shudders, becoming more and more aware of us.

"Mina, stop that," Kai pleads.

Mina ignores him, directing her words at Tristan. "You told Kimberly everything, didn't you? You should be happy that it nearly broke me. You should be *glad.* I could have been out of your life as you wanted."

Tristan takes a step towards her, but Shin blocks his way. "I never said... I never wanted you dead." Tristan and Shin face each other, and I'm certain they're about to come to blows.

Shin's faster. With predatorial speed, he snatches Tristan by the shirt. "You're as sick as your brother!" he snarls into Tristan's face. "I should've known! Pricks like you don't take no for an answer! Take what you want even if the girl is screaming, right?"

Shin's tirade shocks us. "What are you talking about, Shin?" I ask, but a sense of uneasiness crawls over me.

Mina's body trembles violently. I take in her reaction. Her wounded eyes. Her panic when she can't separate the past from the present. Things that didn't make sense start making sense, and yet I still don't want to voice my fears.

Tristan is too stunned to struggle free from Shin's hold. "I've never touched a girl against her will," he says with disgust.

"No?" Shin's derisive tone gives me pause. "Yet you think it's okay to send pictures around of a fourteen-year-old girl being assaulted?"

Did he just say...?

Nate is the one who asks in a careful tone, "What pictures?"

Abruptly, Mina falls to her knees, covering her head with her hands. "Don't!" she shouts. "I don't want to hear this anymore!"

"Kimberly said you showed her a picture of Sean assaulting Mina! Don't play stupid!" Shin roars. His fist flies and Tristan does nothing to stop it, falling hard to the floor. "Where is he? Where's your fucking rapist brother?!"

Tristan's face contorts in a mix of pain and horror, blood dripping from his lips. "Rapist?"

Mina makes a weird sound from her huddled body. Kai reaches to comfort her and Shin screams, "Don't you fucking touch her!" Shin seems to grow larger. "I'll gut you if you touch her! And when I'm done with you, I'm taking out your damn brother! He'll never hurt another girl!"

"Sean..." Tristan wipes the blood from his mouth. "I didn't show anything to Kimberly, Mina." Tristan speaks unevenly.

Nate crouches near Mina, warily keeping an eye on Shin. "Mina, did Sean... hurt you?"

Mina remains silent as Shin goes to his sister. His lips curl. "I swear, I'm going to kill you if you think she asked for it. I can't believe I let you guys get close to her back then."

"Are you saying Sean..." Tristan looks ill. "Did he--? Mina, tell me he didn't..."

"He told us you came onto him," I say aloud. "He said—"

Shin gives me a scathing look. "If you say 'he said' one more time, I'm going to knock your perfect teeth out!" he shouts at me. "He *grabbed* her, you dipshits! He wanted to rape her!"

Oh, God. My stomach churns.

Mina makes another sound, and Shin lifts her head, frowning when he realizes how pale she is. Somehow, he manages to coax Mina into his arms as she begins to hyperventilate. "Come on, Mina. Breathe. You can do this." His words are calm, soothing. "He can't hurt you."

Kai asks painfully, "He raped her?"

Mina's eyes are locked on her brother's as she tries to suck in a breath. When she does, it rattles noisily. "Breathe, Mina." He holds her protectively. "Dad heard her screaming in the woods."

Reeling, I take a few steps back. Tristan's gray eyes fill with tears as he stares at Mina's frail body. It's so much worse than we thought.

Our shock speaks volumes to Shin. "You guys are stupider than I thought," he sneers, rubbing his sister's back. "You think Mina would want someone like Sean? At fourteen? What kind of fucked up minds do you guys have?" He rocks Mina gently, his actions at odds with the harsh voice he directs at all of us. "Dad heard her and found Sean—" Shin breaks off, his jaw moving tensely. "Someone was recording the attack. Sean and the person ran."

I think about the picture: Sean's hands now take on a sinister light. It wasn't consensual. Shit.

"You told her," Mina says, and she sounds horribly young. "You told her I wanted it."

Tristan begins to shake his head vehemently, practically crawling over to her. "No, Mina, I swear."

"Why should we believe you?" Shin demands with a hostile look. "Where's your brother now, Tristan?"

"Harvard," he murmurs.

Shin laughs coldly. "I guess that's where rapists go."

Kai speaks again. "We never told Kimberly anything about Sean. We told her that we thought Mina was responsible for Tristan's dad dying."

Shin makes a rude comment. "Get out. You guys disgust me."

Tristan's voice shakes. "Mina, I didn't know. I'm so sorry."

Shin points at Tristan. "You think you can come here and say you're sorry? Your damn brother tried to rape Mina. She was *fourteen*, Tristan! Do you know what it did to her?"

I shut out all sounds. I should move. I should do something. Console Mina. Help Nate who stands with tears running down his face. But I can't move. Kai's rage breaks us all out of a trance as he swears, slamming his fist into the wall. Blood drips from his hand as he raises his head in anguish.

Tristan slumps to his knees, his face a mirror of devastation.

"Stay away from her. Leave her alone. She's been through enough," Shin says, bringing Mina to her feet. "You know the truth. Get out."

We start protesting. "We're not leaving," Nate says in a choked voice.

"Why the hell not?" Shin nearly shouts at us.

"Because we screwed up!" Tristan roars.

Mina whispers, "It's too late." She walks away from us.

CHAPTER SEVENTEEN

There is chaos around me, but I pretend I'm not there. With childish intent, I leave – or I try to. If I don't see it or hear it, it doesn't exist. The last handful of days have drained my emotional focus. It's easy to be flippant: nearly drowned, my self-harm's been discovered, the mean girls know about Sean. It couldn't possibly get any worse, right?

I know all too well that it can always get worse. So, when Tristan grabs my wrists to stop me, I turn to stare at him. I'm not prepared to see him crying. His body shakes with the emotions warring within him: anger, pain, guilt, sorrow…and something else.

"I'm so sorry, Mina." He pulls me to my feet, enveloping me in his arms and burying his head in my neck. "I'm going to fix this."

"I'm not broken." My voice is harsh and cold, my body rigid and aloof.

"No, but I am," Tristan admits sadly.

"We all are," Nate adds.

Shin starts to intervene, but I shake my head. They're around me, all four of them. I could close my eyes and pretend we're preteens again. "You believed him."

Tristan flinches as I push him away. "I deserve that. If you never forgave me, I'd deserve it. But that doesn't mean I'm going to leave you, Mina."

Shin demands, "What's that supposed to mean?"

I exhale sharply. "And what happens when someone lies

to you again? To any of you?"

Kai extends a hand. "We should have asked questions and trusted you."

I shake my head again. "Hard to do since I never came back to be questioned."

Tristan doesn't wipe his eyes. "No, but we should have talked to you when you came back," Tristan says, reaching for me again. His eyes flicker with pain when I evade his touch.

Mad and angry Tristan is easier to deal with than this Tristan. I don't want to remember the scent of his hair or the way his lips feel against mine. I don't want to remember the curiosity, the flutter of my heart, the tingles of excitement. I don't want any of them to look at me like I'm broken and in ruins.

Lifting my chin, I try to assemble the tattered remains of my pride. "Fine. You know the truth. We can move forward. I just want to be left alone at school."

The Knights look at each other. Eric says, "Not going to happen, Mina. We were part of your life once. We intend to become a part of your life again."

I hiss and my lips thin. "No. You can't just flip the switch by apologizing. It doesn't work that way."

"No, it doesn't." Tristan cocks an eyebrow. "But that doesn't mean we're letting you walk away." When the others nod in agreement, he continues, "We owe you. We're going to make sure no one bothers you."

"It's too late. Kimberly *knows*." I close my eyes. "Everyone will think I asked for it."

"Wait," Shin says. He walks around slowly. "Dad said someone was recording what happened to you, Mina. A girl."

All four Knights exclaim angrily, talking over one another in their haste to get more details. Tristan raises his hand. "Your dad saw a girl recording Sean's attack on Mina?" When Shin nods grimly, Tristan exhales slowly, his gray eyes on me. "We fought that day, remember? You saw Kimberly flirting with me." When I'm silent, he continues, self-hatred creeping into his voice. "I was flirting back because it fed my ego. I was insecure about them," he waves at the other three guys, "mooning about. I thought it would make me feel better if you knew that there were girls who wanted me, too."

Tristan's eyes guiltily connect with mine as Kai growls. Nate smacks his forehead but stays focused on the topic. "If we never mentioned it to Kimberly, then the only way she'd know is if Sean told her or if..." Nate trails off awkwardly.

"If she was there," Shin concludes, slamming his hand flat against the wall

"You are unfreaking-believable, Tristan!" Kai yells. "You flirt with the one girl who's been after Mina from the very first day! All this time we blamed Mina when it was *you*! She hurt Mina because of you! Sean came after Mina because of you! You're the one we should hate!" With each statement, Kai's rage grows.

Tristan steps back with a stricken flinch. "I know that," he whispers, his proud shoulders slumping.

I can't explain what causes me to intervene. "Stop this! You can't just blame Tristan!" I ignore Shin's surprise as I stop Kai from lashing out at Tristan.

"But, Mina," Kai nearly whines, "he started it. It's his fault."

Eric tries to placate Kai. "We need to deal with Kimberly and Sean first!" Eric points out.

Tristan's temper, the one he's trying to rein in and keep under control, flares. "I'll deal with Sean," he snaps, glaring at the other three Knights.

"We all want a piece of him, Tristan! We all have a score to settle," Nate snarls, his anger at odds with his angelic features. "But Kai's right. You brought Kimberly into this shit!"

Shin interposes. "We need to know how Kimberly's involved."

"No!" I shout, startling everyone. "I don't want to deal with this anymore. Just... I want it to go away."

"Mina, Kimberly isn't going to go away just because we

ask nicely," Eric points out. "She talked to you on the boat, didn't she? That was the trigger that caused you to jump?"

I don't respond. I don't have to.

I'm not sure what to expect returning to school after my "accident". When I park my car, all four Knights wait for me in their navy uniforms. As a unit, they walk towards me. Tristan helps me out, Kai takes my bag, Eric closes the car door, Nate opens doors for me. When I try to argue with them, they pull me along like a recalcitrant child. We enter the school as we did years ago: me in the center, the Knights fanning to either side.

Students part like the Red Sea. No one meets my eyes, but a few students glance furtively at the Knights' hard faces. Eric and Nate constantly scan the students for any infraction while Tristan and Kai are rigid with unspoken hostility. I have no idea if they're being overprotective or if they anticipate someone challenging them outright. Aren't they the ones who rule the school?

The moment I see Kimberly, Eric and Nate peel off, blocking her from seeing me but also caging her in. I know they're saying something because Midsummer goes from angry to worried to nervous as she listens. I can't see Kimberly's face clearly – Nate and Eric are tall, after all – but I can make out her high-pitched voice.

Tristan turns me away. "Ignore her," he says, but I catch the way his eyes narrow in anger, and his nostrils flare. He grips my elbow firmly when I slow down. "No, don't. Don't acknowledge her. She's nothing to you. She's nothing."

"We'll be walking you to and from classes," Kai explains when I huff loudly.

"Really, is this necessary?" I ask, craning my neck to see what Eric and Nate are doing.

Kimberly launches herself past Nate and Eric. She's not

alone: Midsummer, Sarah, and Karen are with her. "Did Tristan tell you how he begged us to hurt you and break you, Mina?" she demands. "He promised that if I could—"

Tristan's snarl cuts her off. "That's enough!" He isn't gentle when he grabs Kimberly's arm and shakes her. "You aren't fit to say her name! Do not cross me, Kimberly!"

Midsummer steps forward, but Nate shoves her back roughly. "Don't get involved unless you want to fall hard and fast," he says in a dark tone, smiling when Midsummer pales.

Kimberly remains undaunted, giving Tristan a cocky smirk. "Will she want you when you tell her the truth about us?"

I avert my gaze. Tristan tenses, a muscle in his jaw twitching as he glances at me briefly. "We didn't fuck, Kimberly. I let you blow me. Don't forget how fucking drunk I was before I let you even touch me," Tristan says cruelly.

I blanch at his crude words. "I'm done," I state. I work my way around everyone, only realizing that I don't have my backpack when I'm halfway to class.

Kai and Tristan run to catch up. As Kai hands me my bag, Tristan speaks rapidly, "Mina, this is one of the things I need to talk to you about. It was before I knew you were coming– "

It's been over three years. I know Tristan's been sexually active, but the knowledge is a bitter one. I don't have any right to condemn him, do I? I tilt my head. "You don't get it, do you? I don't care that you had oral sex with the biggest bitch here. You sent her after me. She and her friends hurt me. You started this, Tristan. And now you want me to care and let you help me. How do I know this isn't part of the game? How will I ever trust you? Any of you?" I include Eric and Nate. All four boys swallow. "There's a big gap between forgiveness and trust, and I don't know where I even stand with the first one."

"It's not a game," Kai insists.

Tristan captures my face with a hand. "I know." He breathes the next words into my ear. "No more cutting, Mina. I mean it. Hate me, curse me. God knows I deserve it and more. If you need something to hurt, hurt me. But I can't leave. Not until

I know you're safe." He presses a kiss to my ear.

I jerk away, slapping a hand to my ear. "I am seconds away from committing murder, Tristan," I warn him as Kai growls at Tristan about respecting boundaries.

"I'll take anger over indifference any day, Mina."

Damn him. "I survived without you, Tristan. I don't need any of you."

CHAPTER EIGHTEEN

Mina saw Kimberly flirting with me. I should've put an end to it, but my ego felt good with Kimberly flirting, and Mina looking mad. I'm pretty sure the other boys are going to beat me up when they find out.

I need to fix this, though. I don't want to lose Mina.

"Hey, loser," my brother says when I enter the house.

I flip him off.

"You won't believe what just happened to me," Sean says looking immensely pleased with himself. My stupid brother unlocks his phone and shows me a picture.

It's a picture of him and Mina. They're kissing and his hand is up her skirt. "What the hell is this?"

"She threw herself at me, brother," Sean continues. "Like a tiger. Made me feel her up."

She's fourteen. He shouldn't have touched her. And yet… She wanted him to touch her? Just because I let Kimberly flirt with me?

Her betrayal fills me with grief, but it doesn't take long for the grief to turn to rage. Mina. My Mina. She's a liar, after all.

The memory makes me sick. How could I have been so stupid? Why was I willing to believe Sean? He'd leered at her before. I should've known.

It takes all my willpower to not fly to Boston to beat Sean within an inch of his life. Nate prevails, explaining that Mina's well-being has to take priority. There will be pain for Sean soon enough. I plan to hurt him and break him for what he did to Mina. As soon as Nate and Eric learn the depth of Kimberly's involvement, she'll be added to the list.

Mina's not the same, yet some parts remain. Her quiet genius. I know she's breezing through her classes. The sound of her voice is the same. Soft. Silky. Full of promise.

Her shorter do is still long enough to swing as she walks by. I struggle to focus during class. Surely during the time we've been apart, there must have been guys who drew her attention. Has she kissed anyone else? A surge of jealousy rips through me. It's not fair, of course. I've been with other girls, but that doesn't stop me from being a jerk and wanting to bash every guy she may have kissed.

I try to exile thoughts of her from my head. After all I've done to her, I shouldn't even consider what it would be like to kiss a nearly eighteen-year-old Mina. I shouldn't even think about how much I still want her.

In math class, I watch her. She rarely looks up – in fact, there are times when I'm certain she's bored. When her lips part, I know she's working on homework. She's finishing assignments while good old Mr. Kim is lecturing about differential equations.

After class ends, Nate and I approach her. I don't miss the way she tenses. "After the next swim meet, we're having a get together at my place," I say. "You're invited. If you want."

She blinks. She's so cautious with her words. "A get-together or a party?"

I grit my teeth. The truth is that I'm not inviting anyone else except the other Knights. I just want to see her outside of school. I want her to be around us again.

"Pascal and Eric will be swimming," Nate says.

"Is Pascal going to your gathering, too?"

What's her interest in Pascal? I scowl at her. "No, Pascal's not invited," I say.

She averts her head. I can literally hear Nate pleading *Please say yes.*

"I can pick you up," I find myself saying, "for the competition. You should see Eric swim."

She bites her lower lip. "Why won't you leave me alone?" she mutters to herself. I want to run my thumb over those lips and kiss away the slight frown on her face. "Fine. May I think about it for a day?"

The fact that she's considering it is a win on my part. I pretend it's no big deal. "Sure, whatever."

I don't know what I'm doing anymore. All I know is that I can't stop myself from wanting to be near her anymore. I don't deserve a second chance, but I'm going to do my best to try.

My eyes watch the doors until Mina appears with Pascal, Eric shadowing them with a bland expression. My teeth clench. Is Pascal trying to superglue himself to her side? I'm torn between showing Pascal he's an outsider or kicking his ass. I opt for the former. Once Mina returns to her rightful place with us, he'll see he's not wanted or needed.

It took a bit to convince Pascal to back off on escorting Mina all the time. Eric and Nate had to handle that because I came close to punching the snarky bastard. He apparently didn't get the memo that the Knights are handling everything since he still lingers around her like a lovesick puppy.

"Join us at our table, both of you." I hope it sounds like a cocky order.

Mina and Pascal discuss whether to join us while they grab their food. Eric frowns at their conversation. I can tell Pascal's trying to convince her – I find that surprising. I would think he'd want her to himself because I'm certain he likes her. She's trying to say no. Why doesn't Eric just pick her up and bring her over here?

I'm half-tempted to do that anyway when I see her nod. Some of the tension leaves my shoulders. I'd love to know how Pascal got her to agree. Eric, meanwhile, looks relieved.

Kai stares at the food on Mina's tray. She has a banana and a cup of soup. What the hell? Doesn't Pascal see she's skin and bones? That's when I notice that Pascal has two sandwiches on his tray.

Eric and Nate try to steer the conversation to the mundane. They talk about the swim team with Kai and Pascal, they ask Mina about classes. At first, she barely responds, but as Pascal loops her into the conversation, she opens up. Her dark eyes flit between all of us, and I note a pattern. She stops eating when someone asks her a question. When Eric, Nate, Kai, and Pascal discuss the last swim competition, which I listen to with various levels of interest, she also doesn't eat. But when Eric tells a story about his first swim competition, his words directed at Mina, she begins to work on her soup and then her banana.

She finally finishes her banana – I've never known anyone to eat so slowly before. That's when Pascal places the sandwich on her plate. She wrinkles her nose. Desperate for her to eat her sandwich, I tell Mina about the billiards bet Kai, Nate, Eric, and I had last year. The one who came in dead last was supposed to streak across the football field. I embellish the story for all its worth, digging deep into the details as she takes tiny bites of her sandwich. I know the guys are staring at me with various levels of surprise. My reward is a half-eaten sandwich and a faint smile when she learns that Kai and Eric both had to streak across the field.

"It doesn't surprise me that you won," she then says, and everyone freezes.

I want to shout in excitement. *She's engaging with us!*

"There's the Halloween party I'm throwing at the end of the month," Nate says. "Mina, you're coming, right?"

For a moment, Mina looks sick. She grows pale and her

hands tighten into fists. "No, no, I don't think so," she whispers. Then, without saying anything else, she grabs her lunch tray and leaves.

I shouldn't press her, but I can't help myself. I find her between periods – I know she has a free period in the afternoon – and drag her into one of the restrooms. It's becoming a habit of mine. I lock the door. This time, I notice the way her eyes dart to the door. The flash of panic. When I step towards her, she steps back. Is she afraid of me?

"You're coming this weekend," I state. "After the swim meet."

She licks her lips. "I—I don't know."

I don't stop advancing on her even when she's pressed against the wall. I wrap my hands around her waist. My fingers brush the edges of her hips. "What are you afraid of?"

"Nothing."

She smells good. Why does she always smell so good? I lean a little closer to breathe her in. Involuntarily, my right thumb rubs itself over her throat where her pulse quickens. She may fake indifference, but her body reacts to mine. I hide a savage smile as her eyes flutter close.

Kissing her is a mistake. The action dredges up all my twisted, confused emotions, but it also feels good. When her lips part, I'm not gentle. I want to possess her. I pull her too close and hold her too tightly as desire rushes to every nerve in my body. It isn't until I taste the salt that I see the single tear that's escaped and rolled down her pale cheek. "You're crying? Why are you crying?" I demand. Did I hurt her?

There's so much sadness in her eyes. She shakes her head. "You wouldn't believe me if I told you."

I don't resist when she pushes me away. I don't stop her

when she unlocks the door and leaves me in the girls' restroom.

CHAPTER NINETEEN

Right after Shin "liberated" me from God's Army, I went to these intense therapy sessions. I think they wanted to verify that I wasn't brainwashed by the cult. In my one-on-one sessions, the psychiatrist told me to take everything one day at a time as I adapted to the outside world.

That's what I do now. I have an end in sight, but until then, I take life as it comes. Trying to plan too far ahead only causes me pain.

Seeing them – the four who used to be *my* Knights – bothers me now. There are cracks in my shell of indifference. I'm angry. I'm angry at the emotions Tristan stirred up in me when he kissed me. I'm angry because my heart starts to miss them when they're not around.

"Seriously, is this going to be an everyday kind of thing?" I snark intending to brush by them one morning.

Kai yanks my backpack off, slinging it over his shoulder. Tristan takes my arm gently. "You already know the answer to that."

I sputter as I stumble along. They're serious. Once we're inside, Tristan tucks my hair behind my ear, rubbing a lock between two fingers. "We're doing it because we want to, Mina. We have a lot to make up for." He kisses my cheek.

"I don't need you," I hiss out even if a part of me likes the gesture.

Tristan's eyes are strangely soft. "I know." He tucks my

arm around his and continues to walk as if we're having a normal conversation. "You're stuck with us nonetheless."

Today, Kimberly Moore does not plan to be waylaid. Her eyes flicker to Tristan and then me.

I don't miss the way she swishes her skirts as she walks over. "What is this?" she asks. "All four of them? Are they *sharing* you?" Her lips curl at the way Tristan holds my arm.

"Get out of the way, Kimberly," Tristan says in a cold voice. "I don't want Mina to be late for class."

Kimberly's pale eyes narrow. "We had a deal, Tristan."

"No, we didn't." A muscle twitches in his jaw. "Move before I hit you."

She plants her feet. "Make me."

Nate reacts, grabbing her around the waist and depositing her on top of the trashcan. She shrieks as the students around us gasp. "You're lucky," he tells Kimberly with a smirk. "Kai would've thrown you in there."

"Nate will bring you to math class," Tristan murmurs as we reach my first class.

Kai hands me my backpack. I want to throw a hissy fit. Since that would be childish, I frown and say, "I don't know what game you're playing, Tristan, but I'm asking you to stop."

Tristan's eyes flicker. Eric rests a hand gently on my shoulder. "This isn't a game, little queen. We're here because we want to be." He ruffles my hair, chuckling when I try to swat him.

This isn't right. My chest feels tight as I back away. When I sit in my seat, I glance up to see Tristan and Kai lingering in the doorway. I immediately slouch down as the class whispers around me.

One day at a time, Mina.

Tristan waits for me outside of math class. "Don't frown

so much. What if your face freezes like that?" Tristan teases.

His light-hearted tone affects me more than I want to admit, leaving me off-balance and on edge. I tuck my hair back, frowning at the way my hand shakes, but Tristan simply grabs my hand and leads me to my seat. Nate's grin is cheerful, and I note that they've seated me in between them.

During class, Nate and Tristan look at me periodically while Midsummer observes with hard eyes, texting furiously in the corner. By the time lunch rolls around, I've stopped snarling at the Knights. I do shrug off Tristan's hand – I can stand on my own – but it doesn't stop the gossip mill from spreading.

Each of the Knights brings me a dish they think I'll like. When Pascal quizzically cocks his head at me, I give him a helpless shrug.

"Final swim competition this weekend," Pascal remarks.

Eric's eyes brighten. "Come and watch, Mina. Be our good luck charm." When I hesitate, he puts on his best puppy dog eyes. "It would mean a lot. To me and Pascal. And I can't wait to celebrate your birthday in December."

My face grows blank.

Nate rubs his hands gleefully. "Aww, little queen, remember the parties we threw for you?"

"Don't," I whisper. "Don't bring it up." Memories are the worst because the good ones juxtapose themselves against the bad ones. The moments of carefree mirth against the confines of gray walls...

Nate reaches over with a frown. "Mina, I'm sorry."

I pull my hand back. "You want it to go back to like before. But it can't. I'm not the same. You're not the same." To my horror, my eyes fill with tears. "I've been pushed, shoved, shamed, and bloodied in front of you. Until recently, you were okay with it. It's something we would never have done to each other years ago." Dammit, why am I falling apart now?

It doesn't help that Tristan wraps his arms around me. Somehow, I hold the tears back by blinking furiously even as he murmurs, "I'm here. I'm here now. I'll make it up to you." He grunts when I use my elbow to free myself.

Eric's lips turn down. "What we did to you, what we allowed… It was wrong. But we're trying to make it right."

"Don't forgive us," Kai adds in a gruff tone. "Make us work for it every day of our lives."

Pascal, chewing thoughtfully on a breadstick, says, "At least, now that you have your heads out of your asses, you see your actions for what they are."

Tristan's anger flares. "Takeda, you're here only because Mina wants you here. I have been uncommonly patient about your existence, but you're about to find out that my patience is at an end."

"He's a jealous sort, isn't he?" Pascal asks me conversationally, oblivious to the growing hostility. "What's the matter, Tristan? Worried Mina might prefer someone who isn't a prick?"

Tristan lunges across the table as Kai jumps to his feet. "Stop!" I cry, grabbing Tristan's arm. "Pascal's not interested in me."

"You expect me to believe that? Why wouldn't he be?" Tristan demands, his eyes narrowed with annoyance.

Pascal gives me an innocent smile. "Yeah, why wouldn't I be?" He winks at me. "I don't know, babe. Think we could make something work between us?"

Kai swears loudly, bristling as Pascal chuckles. I shake my head, making an exasperated sound. Tristan watches me carefully as I work to compose myself. "Like I said, Pascal's not interested in me," I repeat.

"We still want to throw you a party," Eric says quietly, "or do something with you. You could even invite Pascal."

Kai's teeth snap shut. Carefully, Pascal says, "You should definitely come to the meet this weekend. I need to skedaddle afterward, but it'd be a treat to see you there. And as for your birthday, I think you know what I want to give you."

Tristan inhales sharply at Pascal's teasing tone. He's being possessive because he wants to be my knight in shining armor again. They all do, and they believe that by doing so, we'll return to our childhood roles again and everything will be fine. A wedge exists between us caused partly by their actions and partly by my reluctance. I need to keep my walls up to finish what I started.

"I'll come," I say, "this weekend."

CHAPTER TWENTY

I slide a headband on and check my reflection in the mirror. My phone buzzes. Tristan texts me again.

Tristan: *I'll pick you up. Nate went early with Eric. Kai will be with us.*

The Knights send a continuous stream of texts all weekend. Nate tells me about driving Eric home after a full body wax – no pain, no gain, right? – where he cried like a baby. (Eric denies this.) Kai sends me texts about a book he's reading.

When I look back in the mirror, there's a slight smile on my face. My cheeks are pink. I look… excited? What am I doing? I can't do this. I have a plan… And yet, the cuts on my shoulder are mostly healed. It would be easy to get another razor…

I look down at my phone again.

Tristan: *Be there in ten.*

I could block these messages, but I don't want to. There's a warm familiarity to them: Eric remembering the cherry lip balm I always used; Kai asking me if I still like coconut cake; Nate eating mac and cheese with hotdogs, our favorite meal when we were twelve.

I decide to think about my plans later. I catch myself humming while I sip my coffee. Shin grins at me while pretending to read a book, taking in my jeans, long-sleeved cotton top, and denim jacket – Canadian tux at its best. He's been doing a few classes online and it keeps him busy. Watching my brother covertly, I think what a burden I've been. "Will you be back for dinner?" he asks casually.

"I-I don't know," I stammer.

He nods. "Just message me. I wouldn't worry about it. Have fun."

When Tristan arrives, Kai jumps out so I can sit in the front. Tristan's gray eyes warm as he takes me in. "You look... nice," he murmurs.

Kai scowls in the back seat. "Your hair is different," Kai adds, flushing when I look at him.

Conversations were less awkward when we were younger, I think idly. I tuck my hands beneath my thighs. I'm quiet despite their attempts to engage me, and eventually, they leave me to my thoughts. I don't mean to be antisocial – actually, that's not true. I don't want to get close to them. I don't want emotional ties.

The moment we enter the aquatic center, the noise and smells stun me. There are a lot of people around, too. To say that I don't go out in public often is an understatement. Tristan notices my discomfiture, gently tugging me towards him with an arm. "It's okay," he says. He cocks his head at Kai so that I'm sandwiched between them. Nate, sitting in the bleachers, takes in our body language with concern.

When we sit, Tristan tucks me next to him before I can give it a second thought. Tristan and Nate explain why Eric and Pascal got waxed yesterday. Supposedly, it's a common thing among swimmers because they believe unnecessary hair causes friction in the water. Nate and Kai argue whether a little chest hair is attractive to women, glancing at me for feedback. I simply shake my head. I'm not wading into that issue.

How do I describe my heart at this moment? A reluctant lightness. For once, I don't feel the weight of my past on me. I'm existing in this moment. With these four boys. The usual weight of guilt and darkness lifts.

Tristan touches my chin gently as Pascal and Eric line up

for their race. Pascal's the faster swimmer, but Eric has better endurance. I should tell Tristan to stop touching me, but I don't.

Nate taps my knee and points because Eric is staring at us. I give this tiny wave and Eric blows me a kiss. The other swimmers notice, and a few guys holler and hoot. Pascal rolls his eyes. With a wink, he blows a kiss, too, before focusing on the race. Tristan huffs, glancing at me.

Across the pool, Kimberly, Midsummer, and Sarah are unhappy with the attention thrown our way. They're with Dustin Clarkson – I think he's a basketball player – and they seem to know one of the other swimmers by the pool. Tristan grabs my hand and places it on his thigh, covering my hand with his larger one. I can't tell if he wants me to feel the muscles in his thigh – which aren't bad – or if he's trying to hold my hand. It's distracting.

"You're blushing," Tristan murmurs.

I yank my hand free. "Look, Pascal is ahead."

Nate leans forward to address me. "You rooting for Pascal? Eric will be sad."

"Final stretch," Kai says.

I feel Kimberly's eyes burn a hole into my body. Kai grabs my other hand in excitement as Eric starts to dominate. Nate is roaring. I'm less effusive as I bite my lip. Eric finishes a fraction before Pascal. Eric is the state champion, but Pascal's right behind him.

Eric checks his time, shouting triumphantly as he pumps his fist before looking at us. I can't stop the smile on my face as we clap enthusiastically. Pascal winks before he and Eric hug each other briefly. I laugh.

"I'm going to the restroom," I tell Nate.

Tristan stops me. "Maybe I should walk there with you."

"You're kidding, right?"

"Fine. But if you take too long, I'll walk in there and clear it out." Tristan gives me a warning look.

In the restroom, just as I get done washing my hands, Kimberly and Sarah enter. I lift my chin as I dry my hands, noting that Midsummer guards the entrance.

"You don't get it, do you?" Kimberly asks me angrily. "Tristan is mine."

"Is he worth all of this?" I ask. "Don't you want someone who wants you back?"

"He does want me," she insists. "He's playing you." She pulls out her phone. "But I'm going to give him the weapon he needs to put you where you belong."

When Kimberly plays the video, I stiffen in horror. Nausea overwhelms me as I hear my fourteen-year-old self crying.

"I can make this go public at any time, Mina," she purrs. "Leave."

No. I'm not going to let her threaten me. I take a moment to gather my thoughts. As much as I want to collapse and cry, I need to keep it together. If she has this video, she was likely the one recording it.

"You were there, weren't you?" I ask.

Kimberly shrugs. "So, what if I was? I'll send it to everyone in school if you don't leave," she says.

"Fourteen is not old enough for consent," I say clearly. "It's proof that Sean assaulted me. And it's unlawful for you to have that. I can go straight to the police with this." I pause for dramatic effect. "You're eighteen, right? That means they can charge you as an adult for possessing this video." I have no idea if that's true, but it sounds legit to me.

Kimberly snaps her mouth shut. Suddenly, Midsummer shrieks as Kai forces his way past her and flings her to the ground. Tristan and Nate enter, fury on their faces. Tristan walks directly to me while Nate corners Kimberly.

Tristan cups my cheek. "Did she touch you? Hurt you?

Some of my bravado fades and I shiver. "No, but…" I bring my head close to his. "Tristan, she has a recording of me…" My voice is barely a whisper.

Tristan's head snaps up, and he turns cold, cruel eyes on Kimberly. Before she can react, his hand whips out, twisting her wrist until her phone clatters to the ground. Nate picks it up while Tristan roughly pushes Kimberly to the wall, his hand at her throat. Sarah and Midsummer cower as Kai looms over them.

Even when Tristan was angry with me, he never looked at me the way he's looking at Kimberly. He wants to kill her. He helps Nate unlock the phone using Kimberly's thumb. "This video," he says tensely before turning to Kimberly. "You were there that day. You bitch." He doesn't raise his voice, but he smiles maliciously when she cries out as he twists her arm harshly. "You make me sick."

Nate disables the password. "We'll be keeping this. I want all copies, Kimberly." Nate's angelic features turn positively wicked. "I'm sure you know my father is well-connected to the DA's office. As this is your phone, Kimberly. It doesn't look good."

Kimberly tightens her lips. "It's on the memory card. That's the only copy."

"It better be, or I will bury you," Tristan purrs. He releases her.

Her smile is sinister. "You always did like it rough. Does Mina know that?"

Tristan raises a hand, smirking when she flinches. "I don't hit girls, but since you're a monster, I have no compunction about hitting you. Stay away from Mina or you'll learn what happens when I lose control. Trust me, you don't want to see me out of control."

We regroup at Tristan's place. I'm curled up in a plush chair, drained and exhausted. Kai hands me a cup of tea with a worried look, but my hand is steady when I take it.

Nate has Kimberly's phone in a plastic bag, and he holds it gingerly, treating the contents as if it carries the plague. "So, what do we do now?" Nate questions, grimacing with distaste.

Tristan rubs his jaw, settling himself near me. He tilts my head up, his gray eyes lingering on my lips. "I want Sean and Kimberly dealt with simultaneously. Sean didn't just assault you, Mina. He took you away from me."

"You could have looked for me," I say bitterly, my eyes sliding away from his.

"We should have," Eric agrees with a grimace.

Tristan runs his thumb slowly against my jawline. "I did," he finally says. The other Knights stare at him in surprise. "I visited your mother to find you."

A shiver runs up my spine. "You... What did she say?"

Tristan swallows. "She told me you wanted nothing to do with me." A flash of remembered pain. "That you saw me as weak and that's why you told your father about the affair."

I close my eyes. I never saw Mom at trial. She pleaded guilty. She wrote us a few letters while we were in Texas, but after the first one, I burned the rest. "I haven't seen Mom since she killed Dad. I spoke to her once. And I didn't tell her about the affair. Dad already knew. He told Shin about it months before... the incident."

Mom, don't leave us here.

Your uncle is your guardian.

Please!

The cup in my hand shakes. "Dad went there that day to find S—your brother. I didn't want Dad to leave, but I was..." I lick my lips. "I wasn't very coherent at the time." I blink back tears.

Kai makes a pained sound.

Tristan inhales sharply before taking the cup from my hand and setting it down. He presses my hands to his chest. "I looked for you because I didn't know how to let you go, Mina. I still don't know if I can. I *will* deal with Sean, I promise you that. He will never hurt you again." His long fingers curl around my hands. "We'll do whatever it takes to make you feel safe."

I look at the other three. Nate and Eric solemnly nod in

agreement. Kai stares at the way Tristan holds my hand with a bleak expression, but after a moment, he nods, too.

The next weekend, when I skip the Halloween bash, no one pries too hard. All four leave the party early, swinging by and throwing tiny pebbles at my window until I let them in. They whine at Shin that they're hungry until he relents and orders pizza for us. We sit on a plush carpet near the fire, eating pizza and playing games. Tristan finds reasons to touch me, his fingers caressing mine as he hands me pizza or helps me stand. If Shin notices, he ignores it, but Nate and Eric exchange glances knowingly. When Kai turns away, I reach out and hold his hand until he smiles at me reluctantly.

CHAPTER TWENTY-ONE

Tristan

In case it wasn't inherently obvious, life has confirmed that I'm an asshole. If it meant that Mina would forgive me, I'd throw myself on my knees and crawl to her. But that would be too easy. She may have softened towards us, but she doesn't trust us.

I want to go back in time. If I could change the past, I wouldn't let the police take her away. Or I would have found a way to keep her with us. Between the four of us, we would have found a way. All her firsts would've been my firsts.

I find Mom busily planning another charity event. "Hello, dear," she says to me without looking up. This is our mother-son relationship: distracted affection.

"We need to talk," I say in a hard voice, slamming my hand on the table so she jumps. I pull out Kimberly's phone and start the video without explanation.

Mom's eyes – gray eyes like mine – widen as she recognizes the two people in the video. I don't need to see the video again. Every second is seared into my memory. It starts with Sean pinning Mina to a tree. She fights like a wild cat. At one point, she freezes, pleading with him. But then his hand reaches beneath her skirt. I don't need to see when he bites her.

"Turn it off!" Mom shrieks, her mouth trembling. "Oh, my God!" She pales so quickly that I wonder if she'll be sick.

"Mina was fourteen when that happened," I say, my disgust clear on my face. The rage within me won't be easily satisfied or contained, but I'm trying to control it the best I can.

Mom weeps. "Did he – did he—"

"No." I listen to my mother's sobs. If Sean had raped Mina, he'd be dead. I would have ripped him limb from limb. To be honest, I haven't ruled out killing my brother. "I'm only going to say this once. I would happily kill Sean if it would bring Mina peace. In fact, I wish she'd ask me to because I'd enjoy it." I let my words sink it. "I'd gladly go to jail and run our names through the gutters to give Mina satisfaction. But she's not like that. So, you have a choice to make. You're either with me or you're not. If you protect Sean, I'm gone. I'll unleash every sordid secret, expose everyone for the monster he or she is. This video goes straight to the police. I'll trash the King family name." I'm manipulating her, I know, because I've always been her favored son. I'll burn the world down for Mina.

"He was always a difficult child," Mom whispers. "Never happy, always demanding."

Sean's trust fund comes from Mom's side of the family, and Mom is the primary executor until he turns twenty-five. My trust fund is from the King fortune and became mine when I turned eighteen.

"What... do you want me to do, Tristan?"

"Cut him off," I say quietly. "You have control over his trust fund and have the right to withhold it. He's committed a crime. I don't want to put Mina through hell by taking this to the police. But I will if it means he goes to jail unless you cut him off. He values money above all things. So, take it away."

Mom swallows. "Your father never wanted him to have the King fortune. I was pregnant with Sean when we married. Your father believed I used my pregnancy to entrap him." Mom averts her eyes. "You care for Mina."

"I love her." I wait for Mom to register my words. "I don't deserve her, but I love her."

Mom ages suddenly in front of me, shoulders sagging. "I'll cut off his funds and lock his accounts."

She agrees too readily. I narrow my eyes. "Don't pay his tuition either," I add. "You'll do this if you don't want our name dragged through the mud. Block his number."

If she's shocked by how much I demand, she doesn't show it. She bites her lip and closes her eyes for a second. Mom values our family name above all things. It's the main reason she put up with Dad's philandering.

When she nods, I'm filled with hate – for myself and my pathetic excuse of a family. My father, who couldn't remain faithful, guilted me and Mina into keeping his affair a secret. But my father didn't deserve such loyalty. In my misguided attempt to be a dutiful and loyal son, I hurt Mina, and that makes me a different kind of beast. My mother only cares about her name and reputation. I suppose she loves me in a fragmented, misguided way, but how she easily accepts dismissing one worthless son for a slightly more tolerable son is telling.

Mina loved us selflessly despite our messed-up families. I am not so selfless.

When Mom excuses herself, I take a deep breath. I've rehearsed this next part over and over. As much as I want to scream and rage, I need to be calm enough to be sure Sean hears every word clearly.

I call Sean.

"What's up, loser?" Sean greets me.

I grit my teeth as bile rises in my throat. I've never wanted to hurt someone so badly before. I falsely believed I hated Mina. I loathe Sean. I want blood. I want his pain. But before that, I need to get my message across. "Don't talk. I know what you did to Mina." Sean begins to say something, but I cut him off. "I said don't talk! I have the video, Sean. She was fourteen, you asshole, and you tried to rape her!"

Silence. Heavy breathing. Then a nasty chuckle. "Yet you blamed her," Sean says snidely. "You blamed your pretty girl, didn't you? What does that make you, Tristan?"

I want to rip his throat out through the phone... God, why did I believe him? I wish I could beat him to a bloody pulp before cutting my heart out and offering it to Mina. "I will destroy you, Sean. You come near Mina again, and I will hurt you.

This is not a threat. It's a promise. Oh, by the way, Mom's cutting you off." Sean screams at me, but I continue relentlessly. "I won't hesitate to make this public if you even *think* about Mina again! I'll uncover every disgusting secret you have and expose you!" That quiets him. "You're getting off easy, Sean. But it's not over. Not by a long shot."

When Sean begins to curse me over the phone, I hang up. I head to the gym and take my rage out there. It isn't enough. As my lungs and hands burn, I realize it will never be enough.

Later, after I confirm my mother has done as she promised, I learn why she agreed so readily: she's received "complaints" about Sean's behavior for years. I explode. It's not just yelling and screaming – I trash the house.

How could she keep that from me? Without realizing it, Mom's betrayed me by hiding Sean's prior transgressions – she's even paid people to keep people quiet. Until Mina, the complaints have been faceless. Apparently, realizing that Sean hurt someone she knew is the final straw. As my mom sobs and begs for forgiveness, I feel something akin to hate for her. I leave before I say something I'll regret, but not before I remind her that I'll happily destroy the King family name. I threaten to find every victim and ensure Mom will never show her face in public again. She simply nods, pleading with me to not abandon her.

All these wasted years. All this wasted energy. I need... Mina. I need to see her and feel her and know that she's safe. I can't snap my fingers and make it right, but I'll be damned if I'm going to give up on what I want. I get how sick that is. The simple fact that her molester is my brother should put me in the *Do Not Touch* bucket. I may be a different sort of monster from Sean, but we have the same pathetic blood.

Mina and I have been circling each other since I kissed her – it wasn't my most shining moment – but it affirmed what

I've always known. I love Mina Steele. I'm hers. It shouldn't have been her job to teach me how to be a better man, but for her, I'll try to be one.

Which is why I'm standing outside of Steele Mansion. I want her to know where I stand. I want her to know exactly how I feel. Of course, I still need to get past Shin and he's a formidable bodyguard. My jaw remembers that all too well.

"No," he says when I ask to see her, noting I'm alone. He doesn't trust me with her.

He blocks me when I try to force my way in. I try to gauge if I can take him. I let him hit me last time, but right now I'm worked up and completely wired. "Shin, it isn't your call. Let me talk to her, for God's sake!" I shout.

"I don't trust you! I don't want her to get hurt!" he yells back at me, getting right in my face.

"I'm not here to hurt her! I'm here because I need her!" I push him. My hands are bruised, and I'm not recovered from my angry fit in the gym, but damn...

"Tristan?"

I'll never get tired of her saying my name, whether it be in anger or pleasure or confusion. Shin and I turn to look at her. She's in an oversized sweater and jeans, her face devoid of the caked-on makeup so popular at Broadmoor. She's perfect in every way. But to be honest, I simply think she's perfect for me.

"I was just telling him to leave," Shin says with an apologetic frown.

"I'm not leaving until we talk, Mina," I say through gritted teeth. These Steele siblings are obstinate.

Mina purses her lips. She doesn't seem thrilled to see me. "It's alright, Shin. I'll talk to him."

"If I come back and she's upset, I won't hesitate to resort to force," Shin snarls. He gives me a final warning look before leaving us alone.

She guides me to a sitting room, cool and composed. Nothing in her demeanor tells me whether she cares what I have to say. "Alright, let's talk." She crosses her arms.

I guess beggars can't be choosers. This is awkward. I came here with a dozen different speeches, but now that I'm here, my mind draws a blank.

"I haven't been a saint these past few years," I begin. Not the best opening line ever.

"I came to that conclusion on my own." Snarky.

I sigh. "You're not going to make this easy, are you?" I forge on before she can speak again. "I messed around. A lot. I never stuck with one girl for long – usually a one-night – "

"Okay, I get the picture." Her nose wrinkles in distaste.

Get a grip, Tristan! "I went for meaningless entanglements, Mina, because I couldn't forget you. Right before I learned you were back, I decided to toy with Kimberly. It fed my ego that she kept trying to win me over. I was drunk. I let her... you know. I didn't have sex with her. I barely touched her. Trust me when I say that I have no desire to repeat the experience." Mina's face is decidedly blank. "I haven't been with anyone since that day. I haven't *thought* of anyone since."

"Great. Thanks for telling me about your sex history." She sounds less than pleased. She's always valued honesty, and that's what I'm trying to give her, but she doesn't seem impressed.

I rub my face in exasperation. "I'm telling you this because I want to be upfront with you. Mina, I'm still in love with you. But you know that already, don't you?" She must have realized it the day I learned how stupid I've been. But Mina's not even looking at me. My voice cracks a little as I forge on. "I'm sorry. I take responsibility for turning the school against you. I was so caught up in myself that I never looked at you long enough to see what you were going through. Every kick, taunt, word – I felt them, too. Not physically. I felt them in my heart. When you were in the water..."

I step closer when she angles her body away from me. "I ran from my grief and turned it into anger. Grief over my father. Grief that you were gone. You were wronged, and I was too selfish and immature to understand that."

I bridge the distance between us so she can see the sincerity on my face. "I'm asking a lot. Not only am I'm related to a monster, but I'm not exactly redeemable myself," I admit. "I tried so hard to convince myself that I didn't love you." Her eyes meet mine, and it gives me the courage to run my fingers over her cheek and press my lips to her temple. "The guys... We made you our queen because you were the strongest. Even when we hurt you, you picked yourself up. You've been through so much, but you're still standing." I don't care if I sound weak as I plead with her. I've come this far, and I'm not about to walk back. As Mina's eyes flutter close, I kiss the tears that squeeze past her lids. "I know there are things you haven't told me, and I'll wait until you're ready. I'm here to be a shoulder to cry on or to be your whipping post. You don't have to hurt yourself. Hurt me instead. Hurt me because of the horrible blood that runs in my veins. I'll be and do whatever you need. But don't ask me to leave. I need to have you in my life in one shape or form because I'm better when I'm with you. Be the one good thing in my life again."

"Stop." Her voice is barely a whisper.

I've let my pride get in the way of the one person who matters to me. There's still an emotional bond between us, and if stop now, I may lose my opening. "Don't cry. Tell me what you need." I'm frantic as her tear-spiked lashes open and more tears spill. Maybe I've misread her cues. Maybe I'm too late.

"Don't do this now." She trembles as I hold her close, her body stiff and resisting.

I tighten my arms around her, ready to release her if she asks again. "Why not now? If you want me to leave, if you want me to stop, you need to tell me why." I'm a glutton for punishment. She needs to reject me outright, and even then, I'm not sure I could walk away.

Mina lets out a shuddering breath, becoming suddenly pliant. "You're not like him. You're not him," she murmurs half to herself.

Her arms creep around my waist reluctantly, almost as if

she can't help herself. It's been too long since I've held her like this, and it feels like home. Instinctively, I kiss the trail of her tears, and then I press tiny kisses to the corner of her mouth. I search her eyes for an objection or protest, but I only find a brightness that takes my breath away. This time, when I kiss her, I'm careful. It's persuasive, gentle, loving. She stirs in my arms, her mouth parting, and I press the heat of my body against her. I kiss her with the longing I've tried to bury within me. The kiss morphs into a needier one on both sides, overwhelming me with heady sensations. Everything about this moment screams heaven, and it's exhilarating. My body wants so more than kisses, but before my other brain can take over, I find the strength to control myself. In my heart, I know I would forgive her for any transgression, real or imagined. She'd only have to ask, and I would because my heart won't function if she's not with me. But I can't rush what's kindling between us. She deserves to be wooed, romanced, swept off her feet. And knowing what I know, I want her to initiate the next step.

Ending the kiss, I pant for a full minute. My other brain is not a happy camper, but this isn't about me. "I hope I'm not imagining this," I mutter.

Her reddened lips curve in a faint smile as she lowers her eyes.

"This isn't another game, love. I'm yours. And I want you to be mine." I cradle her head in my hands. "But the moment you say you're in, that you're mine – I'll hurt anyone that tries to come between us. I'll work every day to be worthy of you." I give in to temptation, kissing her thoroughly until we're breathless again. "Sean's dead to me," I add darkly. "I'll kill him if he comes near you again. I will never doubt you again. I'll do anything and everything to make things right, regardless of the consequences to me."

When she opens her mouth again, I rub my thumb over her soft lips. "Don't say anything right now. Think about it. Think about what you want and what will make you happy." I hesitate. "Talk to Kai, too."

Her eyes flash in comprehension.

"I should go," I say. I note Shin peeking his head around the corner. "And not just because your brother is spying on us." I whisper in her ear, "If I stay, I'm going to keep kissing you. And then I'll want to do more than kiss you. I'm going home to take a cold shower."

Her ear turns red, making me chuckle.

"Let me drive you to school tomorrow. Say yes."

A brief hesitation. "Yes."

When Shin clears his throat, Mina rolls her eyes as I say, "Just saying goodnight." I'm grinning like a fool as we part. I give her a chaste kiss on the cheek before licking the lobe of her ear. Her startled yelp is decidedly intoxicating.

When I get home, I send her a text message. *I love you.*

Mina: *Goodnight, Tristan.*

For the first time in years, I go to bed with a smile on my face.

CHAPTER TWENTY-TWO

Mina

It's obvious that my relationship with Tristan has changed. I mean, I arrive at school in Tristan's Aston Martin DBX – it hasn't snowed yet, but Tristan likes to be prepared. I try to brush it off. Tristan and I live a mile apart. It's environmentally the right thing to do. We can use the nonexistent carpool lane.

Of course, no one buys it for a minute. Pascal teases me relentlessly. Nate and Eric are merely curious, but it doesn't take a genius to see Kai's jealousy and resentment. My four shadows continue to follow me whenever possible, but the dynamics have shifted once again because Tristan is a more present shadow.

He loves me. He loves me still. I whisper it to myself like a secret. It's not a secret. I'm a fool. More than a fool. Will he want me when he realizes how damaged I am? Our hands touch, we brush against each other, we find reasons to walk together. He doesn't kiss me again, but I think he wants to. Instead, he brings me little gifts. A latte in the morning. A scarf.

The need to cut abates a little every day – not that I have a choice. Shin swept my room and bathroom very thoroughly. It's a struggle. Memories creep in like unpleasant visitors, but I resent Shin's search of my bathroom less and less. He checks the white and pink lines daily on my shoulder to be sure I'm not adding any more.

The fall colors fade through November and... I start breathing. The Knights want to do a joint ski trip in December.

Kai's family owns a lodge in Telluride that we can use, and no one thinks it's weird that he'd rather spend time with us than with his parents. There's even a twinge of pleasure as we begin planning our trip.

As Thanksgiving approaches, I decide I'm done with Tristan's offhand relationship. When I settle into the car, accepting my latte, I set it down in the cup holder and look at him expectantly. He gives me a dazzling but curious smile.

"What is it?" he asks gently.

I take a deep breath. Do I want this? The short answer is yes. I want to feel again. More specifically, I want to feel him again. Does that make me weak? I'm not sure I care anymore. I'm not so ghastly thin, and I've gained some weight so my bones don't jut out. And... he did say he wants me. So, I have nothing to lose, right? "You haven't kissed me good morning," I blurt, my face heating when his eyes widen in surprise.

His surprise disappears behind the most cocksure smile ever. "I haven't, have I?" he practically purrs. He leans over, wrapping his hand securely around my neck as he slants his head.

I don't expect a peck, but I'm not prepared for the heat to explode the way it does. He kisses me like he's ready to devour me, and, after a brief hesitation, I kiss him back just as greedily. When his elbow hits the car's horn by accident, the sound jars us to our senses.

"We, uh, should get to school," I say, trying to steady myself.

"We wouldn't want to be late," he agrees in a husky voice.

At school, Tristan shifts from Knight to boyfriend. I guess our morning kiss catapults our relationship into a formal stage. He hooks his arm around my waist as we walk in. When we're in the hallway, Tristan puts the PDA on full blast.

"So much for going slow," Nate snarks at Tristan, bringing

his face close while waggling his brows.

"Go fuck yourself," Tristan snaps.

Eric pretends to clasp his chest in shock. "Such language, Mr. King. Shocking. Shocking, I say."

As the three exchange jibes, I make my way to Kai. I pull him aside, and I know the guys are maneuvering to give us some semblance of privacy.

"Kai, I'm sorry."

His brown eyes shine at me warmly. "For what? I knew it was an uphill battle from the start. That day, when I kissed you..." Shame fills his face. He scans me. "You're... happier. That's the main thing."

I close my eyes. Kai's right. I am happier. How this change occurred so rapidly is beyond me. It just... happened. "There's so much I want to tell you. All of you," I whisper, "but I don't know how." I lay a hand tentatively on his arm. "I don't know if I can." I'm afraid. How will their eyes change when they realize the destruction I've wrought? Will Tristan still want me?

Kai throws an arm around me. "I'm here, Mina." He reluctantly acknowledges Tristan with a dip of his chin. "It was always Tristan for you. Even when we were fourteen," he adds in resignation.

Kai's not wrong. Even at twelve, it was Tristan that brought the flutters of excitement. When vanity hit me at fourteen, it was for Tristan that I primped. And when he said he liked me... I think about the 'what-ifs' – would Sean have left me alone if I'd picked Kai, Nate, or Eric? The questions are fruitless at best.

Before I can respond properly, Tristan stops us in the middle of the hallway, claiming me in front of the students with a long kiss. I want to smack the smirk off his face as students pretend not to gawk around us, and Kai huffs with annoyance.

"Really, Tristan?" Eric snorts, shaking his head. "Maybe you should make her wear a tag that says 'Property of Tristan King'."

Tristan's arrogant features don't shift even as Kimberly

and Midsummer come into view. His eyes rake over them like they're nothing more than worms. "I want it to be crystal clear to everyone," he says, hooking me around the waist.

I should be annoyed, but inside my heart beats harder. It's dangerous because it fills me with want. I'm wavering badly.

After the school day is over, I see Pascal rather than one of the four Knights. "Hey, you," he says, his round face solemn. "Wanted some alone time with you without your four bodyguards."

My lips twitch. "Did you ask them for permission?" I ask sarcastically.

"Seriously considered it, but no, I just gave them the finger and told them to meet you in the parking lot," he says mischievously, laughing with me. "I just wanted to check how you're doing. We haven't had any time to talk privately."

From afar, I see the Knights watching us. They're congregating around Tristan's car and pretending that they're not curious. I scrunch in my jacket and shake my head. "It's complicated, messy, annoying."

Pascal shrugs. "My sister starts here next year. I want this place to be a kinder school than it is now. Besides, you know about me." He follows my gaze. "I'm not the right one to guide you on this. I can only tell you what I know."

"And what do you know?" I challenge him with a tilt of my head.

"For three years, the Knights were the biggest jerks ever," he replies. "They weren't downright cruel or mean. They just didn't care about anyone, Mina. They would never have invited me over to eat with them."

I roll my eyes. "You make it sound like they're my slaves or something. I don't flip my whip, and voila, they love everyone."

That earns a chuckle from Pascal. "No. I meant that you give them a purpose. Something to focus on."

There's bitterness in my tone when I say, "Something that needs to be fixed."

He weighs my words. "Not fixed. Something that reminds them that there are things – and people – worth fighting for. They love you in different ways. Any of them would step up and be *that* guy for you romantically." Pascal pauses as we stop just out of earshot. "But I think only one of them would stop functioning without you."

I look at Tristan briefly "Why did you help me that day?" I ask Pascal.

Pascal's dark eyes are solemn. "Because the look on your face is one that I've seen before – in my mirror. You thought no one saw your pain or what you were thinking? I saw, Mina. Coming to terms with myself, I went through a dark period, too. Your pain was deeper. Worse, maybe. And the ones who were watching were too immature to see the truth. You weren't fighting back because you wanted that pain. That's why I helped you. Because if something had happened back then, it wouldn't be just you that would've been destroyed." He glances at the four now staring at us openly. "It would've destroyed all four of them. That's too many lives, don't you think? You don't think you're worthy, but I know you are. You have a reason now, Mina, to fight. At least four of them."

My mouth drops open. Abruptly, I throw my arms around him, trembling violently. He immediately wraps his arms around me. and we hug each other tightly. I hear a shout in the background, but I ignore it. After a minute, I let him go. He salutes the Knights with a smirk as he walks off.

Nate and Eric are holding a jealous Tristan back, both wearing exasperated expressions. "Does that guy have a death wish?" Kai mutters while Tristan swears out loud.

"He's just a friend," I say with a frown.

"Touchy-feely for a friend," Tristan growls. "I don't want him crushing on my girl."

"He's not crushing on me. I'm not his type."

"What do you mean you're not his type?" Tristan snaps, throwing Nate's hands off.

"Seriously, you don't know?" But when all four of them

get confused, I say, "He's gay. He likes guys. That's why he winks at me when he hugs Eric."

Eric blinks. "Really?" He puffs his chest out, looking smug. "He's got good taste, then."

"You two have been official for less than twenty-four hours and you're acting like a caveman, Tristan," Nate complains. "Can we put a leash on him, Mina? Or an electric collar? When he steps out of line, we can zap him."

I cover my mouth to hide my laughter, but Kai bumps me with his hip, grinning.

Some of the tension leaves Tristan's face as he comes over to grab me by the waist. "Come on, let's go. I'm hungry." His gray eyes lock on mine. "Come back to my place for a bit?"

Pascal's words linger in my mind as I raise my hand to Tristan's face. "Yes."

CHAPTER TWENTY-THREE

Strangely, we settle into a semi-familiar routine around the Steele siblings. For Thanksgiving, we abandon our parents – not difficult to do since most of them are too busy with their hoity-toity social circles – and congregate at Steele Manor.

The original plan was to prepare dinner for Mina and Shin. Nate and Eric do the grocery shopping, Tristan and I watch tons of YouTube videos. It shouldn't be that hard.

Mina and Shin watch with curiously benign expressions as Nate discovers a potato peeler and Tristan cuts himself on a knife. Eventually, Mina hops off the table while Shin finds a Band-Aid for Tristan.

"Here," Mina says, helping Nate position the peeler while holding the potato at an angle. "It's easier if you move it away from you." She demonstrates and then guides Nate's hands to mimic the action. After he starts peeling to her satisfaction, she piles the potatoes and carrots for him to finish.

Tristan watches her with lidded eyes when she approaches me. Knowing him, he's probably finding something hot and sexy about her instructions. Taking an onion, she instructs me how to trim it and cut it in half before cutting it into small pieces. She then grabs two of the newly peeled carrots and shows me how to chop without losing fingers in the process.

"Thanks," I say. "I'd like to keep my fingers." Her laughter is warm as I bask in her attention. It's the Mina I remember all too well.

Shin provides first aid to Tristan while Mina observes me

for a minute before helping Eric with the turkey. I try to recall if Mina ever cooked when we were younger.

"I'll help Eric with the turkey," Shin offers, "if you want to get the pie started, Mina."

Mina nods, washing her hands and pulling out bowls like a pro. She sets Tristan to cutting apples after showing him how to use an apple peeler – who knew such contraptions existed?

"Now what do I do?" Nate asks, staring at his bowl of peeled potatoes.

I'm about to call him out on his deliberate cluelessness until I see his face as Mina tells him what to do. He's basking in her attention as much as I am. His eyes linger on her fondly as she hands him a pot.

When she starts working on the pie crust – seriously, without a recipe? – Eric doesn't hide his surprise. "Mina, have you been training to be a chef or something? When did you learn to cook?"

Her dark brown eyes meet Shin's as a myriad of emotions crosses her face: fear, sadness mixed with darkness, and horror. Shin's eyes fill with something else: empathy, compassion, and pain.

Has Eric opened a can of worms? He begins to stammer an apology when Tristan rises, wiping his hands off on a towel. He sweeps Mina into his arms from behind, resting his head gently against hers. "What is it, love? You can tell me. You can tell us."

Mina and Shin continue to stare at each other until a faint shake of her head causes Shin to look away first in disappointment. "It's nothing," Mina says. It's obvious she's lying, but why is she lying?

When Mina returns to the crust, Nate smoothly changes the subject. "I thought you needed to chill the crust first."

Pushing the hair away from her face ineffectively until Tristan does it for her, she says, "With a butter crust, yes. But shortening allows you to cheat a bit." She's regained her composure and manages a smile. Tristan refuses to leave her side, though, holding on to her as if he can inject his strength into her body. The jealousy and envy I normally feel are still there, but I can't deny that Mina is better. It tempers my negative emotions.

Eric and Nate allow their shoulders to relax as Shin and Mina continue to pass out orders and requests. The awkwardness fades as we become echoes of our younger selves.

Nate sighs as he sits back, patting his stomach. "All that work and we demolished it in an hour," he says.

"When I said to add a stick butter to the mashed potatoes, how much did you add, Nate?" Mina asks thoughtfully. She's been looking at the potatoes a lot during dinner.

"Those were amazing mashed potatoes," Eric points out. He's had at least two servings. I've had three.

"I added the stick you gave me," Nate replies.

Shin tastes the potatoes again and quirks an eyebrow at Nate. "Well, she handed you the box of butter."

Nate guilelessly nods. "Right. The stick."

Tristan's eyes grow wide. "You added a whole box of butter?"

Mina chokes on her laughter. "There are four sticks in a box of butter."

"You don't know the difference between a stick of butter and a box of butter?" I ask.

Nate turns red. "I do. I mean, wait."

"Well, it was delicious," Eric says. "And super buttery."

We can't stop laughing, but we settle down when Mina serves the apple pie. Tristan settles Mina on his lap and feeds her. Her light laugh makes me smile. It's intimate, yet it doesn't faze any of us as we watch them.

"If you don't mind, try not to get too handsy with my sister while I'm around," Shin says with a grunt. "The last thing I need to see is my sister making out with her boyfriend."

It doesn't escape anyone that Shin's acknowledging Tristan as Mina's boyfriend. It makes it super official.

Tristan chuckles as we stand. Thankfully, Shin has the help cleaning after us – I'm so tired from cooking that I don't think I could clean even if I wanted to – so we immediately retire to watch movies. Mina's never been a typical girl. She's comfortable watching action flicks and horror movies, and we decide on a zombie-themed marathon starting with *World War Z.*

"I hope we all age as well as Brad Pitt," Shin says.

"I hope I'm never dumb enough to keep calling someone on a deadly mission," Eric says with a sigh as zombies attack the soldiers in the movie while Pitt's character tries to silence his phone. "And what is wrong with putting your phone on vibrate?

I add, "I hope emergency phones are smaller than that thing they gave Pitt's character."

We continue to pick apart the movie.

"There's no way you would survive a crash like that," Tristan murmurs. "Look at the way the plane broke apart."

"At least we're not arguing about whether or not Jack and Rose could have fit on that wooden door together in *Titanic,*" Nate says. We fought about that for an hour.

Tristan agrees. "And we all know that Jack could have climbed on top of Rose." He holds Mina close. "Body heat is perfect for warming up."

"Okay, you can stop that," Shin complains, throwing a pillow Tristan's way.

Mina glances my way, wrinkling her nose a bit before we both burst into laughter.

CHAPTER TWENTY-FOUR

Mina

Mina

We get our first flakes of snow in early December. My birthday looms, but I cannot honestly say whether it is in a bad or good way. It simply is. Tristan is… I want him. My plan is falling apart, and I'm not sure if I care.

"A small, tiny birthday party. Just us, the guys, your brother. Pascal, if you want." Tristan punctuates each request with kisses. It's a few days before my birthday, and he's doing his best to be persuasive.

I want to stay here, like this, and maybe dark thoughts won't force their way in. We're cuddling in his bed, and it feels perfectly normal. A content warmth fills me.

"I've never brought a girl in here before," he continues, his lips on my neck. "Only you. This is the only place I let all my guards down." He stops when he notices my silence. "What's wrong?"

My eyes fixate on the ceiling. Tristan's room has an almost beachy-like feel: wood-paneling, open spaces, hues of blue and green. I want to stay here, which is precisely the reason why I shouldn't. I need to leave. I need answers before I make my decision. "Would you take me home?" I ask without answering him.

Tristan sits upright. "Mina?" There's an edge to his voice. "Is it because I talked about other girls?" He ignores me when I shake my head. "I never cared about them, Mina. You're the only one." He cradles my face. "I won't mention it again. I love you. Only you."

"It's not that."

Confusion and pain fill his eyes. "You're not getting rid of me that easily, Mina. I don't deserve you and maybe this is payback, but if you think I'm walking away from us every time you push, think again."

His moves off the bed, extending his hand coolly to me to help me stand. "I'm here, I'm yours whether you want me or not." Without warning, he pulls me against his chest. He doesn't ask before he kisses me hard as if to remind me of what exists between us.

We don't speak during the drive home. As soon as we arrive, I leave without speaking, intent on finding Shin. Tristan calls my name repeatedly – probably with growing exasperation – but I continue, calling for my brother. I find him in the kitchen eating a Twizzler. I come to such an abrupt halt that Tristan bumps into me.

My brother looks at me, tensing. I tell him, "I want to visit Mom before my birthday."

Tristan stiffens as my brother's eyes go from me to Tristan. Shin takes in the set of my chin and nods. "I'll get it arranged right away." Shin sounds his usual even-tempered self.

That's when I finally address Tristan. He probably thinks I've lost my marbles. "I want you to be there." I pause. "I need you to be there."

Tristan considers me carefully, the irritation leaving his face. "I'll be there."

Mom was tried for second-degree murder, but as the case dragged, she was offered a plea deal for voluntary manslaughter. The jury found her unsympathetic and vain, but since the only people there at the time were Mom, Dad, and Mr. King, the prosecution feared she would play the "crime of passion" defense. Since Tristan's father had not been faithful, it would have been easy to bring in a string of mistresses to testify how much Tristan's dad strayed.

There's something stark about the correctional center as it stands unpleasantly against the world. There are families. Individuals. Some are sad, others happy. The cacophony of sounds fills me with bleak unhappiness. Mom killed people. She deserves to be here. And yet, a part of me yearns to connect with her.

Tristan's visited my mother once to glean details of my new life only to encounter more lies. I'm aware that I might get the same treatment, but I'm prepared. We're taken to a private room with a monitor. I foolishly think about the gray wool dress I'm wearing – it seems like a drab choice, all things considered.

Tristan sits to my right, holding my hand under the table. If he notices that my hand is cold and clammy, he remains silent on the issue. Shin, to my left, places an arm around my shoulder.

When Euna Steele appears, Tristan tenses slightly. She's smaller than I remember. In my mind, I still expect to see her in her designer clothes, not an orange jumpsuit. I remember the fights she and Dad had about her wardrobe budget. Since we had to submit our names for clearance, she's not surprised to see us. Her hair is short and frizzy, coming barely to her shoulders, and her orange jumpsuit makes her skin seem sallow and sickly. She's applied makeup to hide the passage of time, but the woman I see is a caricature of who she used to be. The makeup, garishly applied, makes her seem older than her forty-three years.

"I did not expect to see all three of you together," she says as soon as the guard secures her to the chair and then steps back. "It looks like he found you despite everything."

I'm grateful that she is not physically in front of us. Her black eyes look at me carefully before lingering on Shin, then more briefly on Tristan.

"Tristan didn't find me," I say shortly. "You made sure of that. Shin and I are back because of the inheritance."

She shrugs. "Of course. My in-laws hated me. I was surprised they left everything to you, Mina." Then towards Tristan, she says, "Obviously, that makes Mina a worthy catch, don't you think? I never did like you and Mina together, but now I see you won't let her now that she's so wealthy."

Tristan doesn't respond, keeping his eyes focused on me. "I came here to ask you a question," I say.

My mother shrugs again. "Yes, why else would you come to see me?"

I clench Tristan's hand tightly. "What happened that day?"

When Mom smiles, it isn't entirely pleasant. She looks at Shin again before replying. "I wondered when you would ask. I knew it would be you since everything is your fault. I told you to stay away from the King boy, but you wouldn't listen."

"Why?"

She pretends to look at her nails. "How strange to talk about this now. Baron loved me. How strange it would be if you two were together when we got married."

"My father was not going to leave Mom to marry you!" Tristan spits out. "You were nothing but another woman he used!"

My mom's lips turn down. "You don't know that!" Her raised voice causes the guard to shift uncomfortably. After glancing over her shoulder, she leans towards the camera. "We don't have much time. Your father came in and saw me with Baron. That's all."

I close my eyes. "You can't incriminate yourself twice. I want to know what happened in that room."

"Why? It won't bring you peace," she sneers.

Tristan vibrates with resentment next to me; surprisingly, he keeps his temper under control.

"Your *father* came in complaining about Sean. Baron didn't care, but he wouldn't stop." My mom's painted lips twist. "Derrick didn't even care that I was with Baron. All he cared about was you, Mina. I left and got the gun in my bag. I wanted to scare your father, make him see I didn't care about him either. But he and Baron were fighting when I came back. Baron said he would talk to Sean, but Derrick said it wasn't enough. Derrick was not interested in the money. He was going to call the police. Can you imagine the scandal? I fired at him to stop."

The story sounds too simplistic, too abrupt, but I doubt she'll tell me more. I wonder if she simply wanted to get rid of Dad.

"Is that when Dad died?" Shin asks, speaking for the first time.

"I don't know if he was dead then. I didn't check. He was bleeding." Her callous words are horrifying. "But Baron. He wouldn't help me. He said it was all on me. He just stood there and told me I was on my own."

Tristan's hard voice stops my mother from continuing. "You shot him then?"

My mom blanches. It's the first sign of regret. "Yes. I was tired of being second best."

I suspect that Baron's rejection of her fueled her action. Inadvertently, it was a crime of passion – but of a selfish one from a narcissistic woman. She lashed out at a man who had no intention of running away with her.

I block Mom's view of Shin and Tristan by leaning into the camera. "Why did you send us to Uncle Soong?"

Mom raises an eyebrow. "He was family."

Shin says, "Yes, he *was*. Did you know about him when you sent us?"

Tristan's hand twitches. This is the first he's heard about an uncle.

Mom stares at us silently, and she seems sad. "I did not mean for you to be there, Shin."

Of course. I let out a harsh laugh. She has my pity, but she'll never have my love. "No, you just wanted me there." Shin squeezes my shoulder. "I have what I need." I gesture to the guard that I'm done, ignoring Tristan's questioning look. "There's nothing else for me here."

"You'll visit me again, Shin?" Mom demands.

Shin glances at her briefly and shakes his head.

"What is it about you, Mina? Why do they abandon me for you?!" Mom shrieks, the guard holding her when she tries to lunge at the camera.

I shut out her words, focusing instead on the concern in Shin's eyes and the love in Tristan's touch.

On the long drive home, I lean my head against Tristan and remember.

I'm kept in isolation during my period. This is important, Jesus says, because it is proof of my fertility. I am punished because I called Uncle Soong by his false name, not by his reborn name, Archangel Michael. My uncle tells me that Jesus is truly benevolent and careful with the girls chosen. If we are bred too soon, a traumatic birth could impact our fertility. That's why they wait until we're at least sixteen. They are waiting for me to turn sixteen.

I peek out my window and I see Shin working the fields. He's strong. They want him in the army. Jesus says he might even be one of the lesser angels, reincarnated. Shin's face is stoic when one of the women walk by, weeping. He doesn't look on in pity. Has he changed? Will he care when I'm dragged to the altar and given over to the men? I'm watched too carefully by everyone. No sharp objects. I'm given chores that don't require them. As I stare at my brother, I can't feel an ounce of hope.

CHAPTER TWENTY-FIVE

"Are you sure this is a good idea?" Kai asks for the umpteenth time.

I grit my teeth. "Shin said it was." If I'm being honest, I don't know if a little "party" is a good idea or not. Mina might get upset.

Eric and Nate send the caterer away. "Easy! If she gets mad, we blame Shin," Nate points out helpfully. He's annoyingly cheerful. He goes back to check the coconut cake that was custom made for her: white cake layers filled with pineapple curd and topped with toasted coconut flakes.

After a lengthy debate, we decide not to invite Pascal for the first half of the party. It's important to us that we have this private moment with Mina and Shin so we can be open with Mina. We're bridging the gap, hoping she'll take our hands and trust us again.

My present for Mina weighs heavily on my mind. Will she reject the gesture? I was surprised she initiated the next step. Now that the door is open, I'm not one to hold back.

Mina's mom makes my mother seem like a saint. There are questions I want to ask, but is she ready to answer them? The reason Mina sought her mother out remains unclear, but I know now that Derrick Steele didn't confront my dad about the affair. He died protecting his daughter. He died fighting for her, but it won't be in vain.

Dad knew about Sean – he knew Sean was a monster and allowed him to be near Mina. He tried to buy off Derrick Steele.

(We know that Evelyn Steele kept a tight leash on Derrick Steele's spending. Considering Euna's greed, I can see why that was done. But Derrick Steele still stood to inherit his parents' wealth.) Dad tried to cover Sean's *crime* against Mina because he believed in money over the wellbeing of an innocent girl. The pangs I once felt about my father dissipate. The fact that I held his death against Mina makes me sick.

We have a heavy debt to pay to Mina and Shin. Shin's borne the weight alone: caring, protecting, defending. We should have been there along the way.

"I still want to know what happened in the past three years," Eric says, checking the flowers in the vase. There is a rose in there from each of us: yellow from Nate, white from Eric, pink from Kai, and red from me.

I want to know, too. There's a darkness that comes to Mina's and Shin's eyes at times –darkness that comes from the years we were apart.

Nate runs down the steps. "They're here."

I reach for the door before Mina can ring the bell. For a few seconds, all I can do is stare at her. She has a cream cloak draped over her shoulders. Underneath, she's wearing a wrap dress in the darkest red.

"Asshole, it's freezing out here," Shin snaps, pushing his sister in.

I recover, collecting Mina in my arms to warm her body. The sharpness of her body has softened now that she's eating regularly, and the soft swell of her breasts and curve of her hips are distracting. She doesn't need to be warmed, but I relish the feel of her body against mine and allow my fingers to linger on her waist. I steer my brain away from what I want to think about.

The other three guys pop out as I bring her in. Her brown eyes go quickly to Shin. I can tell from that glance that she suspected that we would all be gathered here. She's carrying a white shopping bag, which Kai takes from her and sets aside.

"I know you said no party, but you're eighteen and we

need to celebrate with you." I lift her head. "I need to celebrate with you." I place a chaste kiss on her lips. She doesn't seem angry or upset. Since the day she demanded to see her mother, she's been more aloof. Patience is not my forte, but I'm trying hard not to push her.

"We each got you a little something," Eric says, and the way Mina raises her eyebrows, I can tell she doubts the "little something" Eric mentions.

Eric goes first, handing her a white box with a huge silk ribbon. Feeling possessive, I sit next to her, running my hand down her back as she opens the box. Inside, Eric has framed a sketch done in charcoal. It's of Mina's tree house-castle that we built and designed with her. But he's taken it one step further. He's drawn us as we were back then: Kai tying the swinging rope; Nate on the lookout; Mina and I holding hands at the base of the tree; Eric looking at the world.

Mina's fingers tremble over the drawing. "Thank you, Eric." Shin watches her carefully as her mind relives memories only she can see. Biting her lip, she sets the drawing aside with careful precision.

Kai and Nate hand Mina an envelope. "This is from both of us," Kai says, but when Mina reaches for the envelope, he grabs her hand in his. They exchange a solemn look. Neither Mina nor Kai has mentioned it, but I suspect Kai believes he crossed a line. It's the only explanation I have for Kai not pursuing Mina because he still wants her.

Once Kai releases her hand, she opens the envelope to find our Christmas itinerary inside. We'll be going to the Reeves lodge in Telluride on a private plane that Nate's secured. A strange look crosses Mina's face, but it disappears quickly. "All of us?" she asks, sliding a glance at her brother.

I place my hand on her knee. "All of us."

I then bring my box over. Inside, she finds two jewelry boxes. I point to the slightly bigger velvet case. "Do you remember the ring you made from our hair?" I ask her. When her eyes widen, I continue, "I kept it, Mina. I couldn't let it go." She opens the jewelry box to find a locket hanging from a platinum chain. Opening the locket, she finds the hair ring nestled inside.

"You kept it all these years," she murmurs half to herself.

It's a risky gift because she entwined our hair when our feelings were still honest, pure, and untainted by the world. Since then, I've hurt and betrayed her. I want her to know that I'm capable of seeing our relationship with a purer lens, even if I want more than just a few kisses.

I tap the second box, trying to hide my nerves. Inside, nestled in the cushions, is a platinum ring with a round Australian opal glittering with shades of red, blue, and green.

Shin swears. "If that is what I think it is, I will kill you, Tristan!"

Mina's startled eyes meet mine. "It's a promise ring," I say quickly. I show her that it fits on her pinky. "A promise to never doubt and to be faithful to the two of us. And maybe one day, I'll be able to give you a different kind of ring." I say the last few words softly, a thrill moving through me when she blushes. She takes a moment to look at the ring and then Eric's drawing.

"Thank you. All of you," she whispers. Her eyes go to her brother. "There's something I need to tell you… all of you. Even you, Shin." She pauses. "Shin, I read the will." When her brother freezes, she says, "The conditions of my inheritance are that I go to Broadmoor Prep and live at Steele Manor until I'm at least eighteen."

I look at Kai with a frown. What does that have to do with anything?

"Mina," Shin begins, and it's so rare to see him off-balance. "I didn't mean to keep that from you. I was worried and desperate. I wasn't trying to deceive you."

Mina's lips twist faintly. "I know. And I'm not angry. I know why you did it."

Shin glances at us nervously. "So, we're okay?"

"What's going on, Mina?" I ask.

She takes a deep breath. "I know you're curious about what happened to us after we left here." Her eyes are still on her brother. "I think now's the time to tell you."

Nate sits down next to Eric. "We're listening," Nate says.

Strangely enough, Shin takes over the narrative. "Mom sent us to live with her brother."

We always thought Euna Steele was an only child. I didn't know there was an uncle until Mina mentioned it while talking to her mother.

"He lived in Texas," Shin goes on, his eyes still on Mina. "Mina was still in shock and processing what happened when we arrived. I don't remember much of the trip, but we drove out to the middle of nowhere. Have you ever heard of God's Army?"

Eric pipes up, "Yeah, it was a cult in Texas..." His voice trails off as a chill runs up my spine.

"Uncle Soong was part of it." Shin ignores Nate swearing. "Except he went by Archangel Michael."

I know about God's Army. It was a cult where the leaders kept young girls and women, forcing them to bear the "archangels'" children. As soon as that thought enters my mind, I grab Mina's chin. "No, no, tell me they didn't," I plead, but her eyes tell me nothing.

"The girls had to be at least sixteen before they could be inducted into God's Army." Shin's voice becomes emotionless and flat. "Until then, they were groomed to become future breeders."

Mina jerks her chin away and refuses to meet my eyes, but there's harsh set to her mouth. "I was rescued before I turned sixteen, Tristan."

I explode off the sofa. "Did they *hurt* you?! Did they—" I can't finish the question. I collapse to my knees, grabbing her hands. I don't know what to do. "Look at me, Mina. Please."

Eric lowers his head, biting back tears, but Kai speaks for us. "What else, Mina? What else happened?"

Again, it's Shin who answers. "I got them to trust me. I escaped. A group of do-gooders leaving water for people crossing the border found me. The FBI, the ATF, Homeland Security. They all wanted a piece of God's Army. They planted stories about finding a body matching my description to make the leader think I was dead. I knew where Mina was, but it took over two months of planning before we were able to rescue her." He closes his eyes. "There's a price to everything."

Mina finally looks at me. "The women and men were housed separately, so I didn't know what Shin was doing. They told me he died."

"They punished her," Shin says, but I don't have the energy to look at him.

Mina stands, unbelting her dress and sliding it half off before I can stop her. My first instinct is to cover her – I don't need the guys gawking at her body. But she stops the dress from completely exposing herself. On her left shoulder, I see the pink scars from her self-inflicted cuts right before she turns so we can see her upper back.

Against her pale skin are scars – some faint and a few that aren't – crisscrossed in no definable pattern. *They punished her.* That's what Shin means. They beat her, whipped her. My mind can't stop the images that invade. They beat… a child. Mina. My girl. The world fades in a haze of red.

Robotically, Mina shrugs back into her dress, retying it at her waist as if she didn't just nearly undress in front of us. Normally, I'd be distracted by the flashes of her skin, the exposed curves. But right now, I need to know she's okay. The helpless rage makes me tear at my hair. I want to howl and scream and destroy something, *anything.*

For a while, we're deathly silent until Mina says, "Hope came and went, but Shin was all I had."

No, you had us, too, I want to say. But she didn't. We weren't there.

"For the first time, hope didn't come back. I stopped wishing for…anything." Mina speaks quietly. "I stopped looking at the stars, hoping one of you would come and save me. And I realized that all I do is brief grief and death. Dad, Tristan's dad, my brother."

Kai's choked cry cuts through my anger. He's crying,

openly. Nate doesn't make a sound, his eyes shadowed with regret as tears streak down his face. Shin buries his face in his hands as Eric rests a hand on Shin's shoulder. Eric wipes at his tears, looking at me.

"By the time the compound was raided…I broke. I shattered." Mina exhales slowly. "It took a while to piece myself together. I know, it's my birthday and we should be considering happy thoughts, but…" She splays her hands expressively. "This is part of my past now."

The media covered what happened to God's Army. The government laid siege on the compound. The woman in charge of the girls had dug a hiding spot and partial tunnel for the girls over the years. The story gets muddled about whether she expected an Armageddon-shootout or if she was trying to dig her way out. She was an unwilling follower. When the shooting began, the women hid underground, hoping and praying that they would be freed. The cultists, looking for their women, thought they had somehow escaped. When the agents entered the compound, the men had killed themselves. Except for one older woman, who had stayed out in the open to provide a cover story and was bludgeoned to death, all the women and girls survived. I recall reading about the survivors: a few babies and young children, a 15-year-old girl, two 18-year-olds, and a handful of women ranging from twenty to forty.

I understand why Mina wanted to see her mother. She wasn't looking for details on the day Euna Steele killed Derrick Steele and then my father. Mina was trying to ascertain whether her mother deliberately sent her to her crazed uncle. There's a reason why Mina wants us to learn this today.

It comes to me in a flash of insight. She knows her mother never properly loved her. Mina adapted when she was younger; she found us. But when we were tested, she found us wanting. Her entire life she's been repeatedly rejected or hurt by those who should've loved her.

This is our second test and our second chance; if we blow it, there won't be a third. She'll walk away from the Knights and even from me. She doesn't need to say it for me to know it. I push aside my needs. This isn't about me. It's about Mina and what she needs and what she wants.

I stand and pull her to her feet. "You've never brought grief, Mina. You taught me to love." I take her hand and rest it against her heart. "This, Mina, has always been the strongest part of you." I move her hand to rest over my heart. "You're not broken or flawed. You feel this? You made me whole at twelve. You make me whole at eighteen. Even when I thought I could move on, I wanted to find you because this heart only beats for you. I trust you with all of me because you're perfect. For me. I won't fail you again." I don't want one night, one month, or one year with her. I need her for all my days to come. "Whatever you need, I will be whatever you want and need."

Her lashes grow spiky. A movement to my right causes me to shift, but I'm not relinquishing her hand by a long shot. Kai looks at the ceiling for a moment like he's gathering his thoughts as he tries to dry his face. "Dumb jock. Brute. I've been called all those names. Remember teaching me how to read?" he asks Mina.

My eyes widen as Mina dips her chin. When did Kai not know how to read?

"You never judged me." He exhales slowly. "You were patient. And you saw me as more than a dumb jock. You made me feel smart and valued. You made me a better person. I lost that when you were gone. I know you've been through a lot. Sean. Whatever the fuck that army thing was." His brown eyes settle on her face, but after glancing at me, he wisely doesn't touch her. "You could have disappeared, Mina. But you came back because your heart is bigger and because you're braver. You did it for Shin. So, no, I'm not walking away. Whatever you've been through, we'll deal with it together."

Nate steps up. "You make us a family, Mina, and families don't leave. It took us a while to understand that. We're sorry. I'm sorry. But Tristan's right. We're not walking away ever again. We'll be your rock because you've always been ours."

While Kai and Nate are respectful of my possessiveness, Eric is not. He steps behind Mina and hugs her, ignoring my heated glare. "We love you, Mina. It took us a while to grow up, but it doesn't change how we see you or feel about you." He runs a finger along the back of her hand, smirking when I rip his hand away. "This is just a shell. Your soul, your heart, everything inside -- it's still the same. You're processing a lot of pain, but you don't have to do it alone. We're here. We'll carry you when you're too tired and help you find your way back. Even if you have a jealous, insecure boyfriend. And when he screws up, we'll be here to beat the crap out of him."

This earns a faint laugh from Mina, but then she bites her lower lip with a glance at Shin. This time, she lets the tears fall slowly. "I couldn't find my way back," she finally says with a shaky voice. "So, I set an end date to focus on. I wasn't sure if I wanted to keep living like this."

I suck in a harsh breath. Eric closes his eyes briefly, Nate's mouth twists in pain, Kai rests a hand on Mina's shoulder, and Shin muffles a sob. I bring her hand to my lips, kissing the limp palm fervently.

I don't stop kissing the palm of her hand, needing to feel the warmth of her skin and the softness of her touch. "I lost hope, too. That's why we belong together, Mina. Because hope returned with you."

Shin considers my words. "Maybe you can find hope again, Mina. It's here. With them. With me." Mina's eyes widen.

"Group hug?" Eric suggests. "I think this calls for a group hug."

I growl, Kai groans, and Mina giggles. Nate and Eric take that as their cue to pull Shin in. Mina's in the center, wrapped in my arms. Shin hugs her from the side, Eric from behind, and Nate from the other side. Then Kai wraps his huge arms around the whole mess.

"I love you, Mina," I whisper, not caring that everyone can hear. "Happy birthday."

CHAPTER TWENTY-SIX

In life, we are rarely given second chances. We screw up, we part ways, we move on. Sometimes, we never think of our mistakes again. That would not have been our story with Mina. Even if she had never appeared, eventually we would have looked for her. I believe that.

After Mina's birthday, the dynamic morphs again. We are no longer children playing games. I no longer feel a twinge of jealousy watching Tristan's relationship with Mina deepen. Instead, I'm protective of their relationship. I'm protective of the happiness and pleasure they bring each other.

Even without asking, I think Eric and Kai feel the same. In the end, we're united in our goal of giving Mina back the happiness she deserves.

One thing I wish I could do over is our entanglement with Kimberly and Midsummer. Since commandeering her phone, Kimberly's been AWOL, which is fine by me. But all good things must come to an end.

"So, what's the plan after high school?" Pascal asks us during lunch. He usually has lunch with us but having entered a relationship with some guy named Zayd, Pascal's often gone as soon as school is over.

Tristan's favorite lunch activity is offering Mina little bites of food. It's both cute and sickening at the same time. He offers a carrot stick to Mina. "Mina and I applied to Beaverton Institute of Technology." Using another carrot stick, he points at Kai. "I know you're thinking of playing soccer at Beaverton

University."

Eric and Kai exchange glances. "We're both thinking of BU, but I hate the thought of us going to different schools."

"They're not that far apart," Mina says, digging into the crème brûlée. "Nate?"

Mina never forgets to include each of us in conversation. "BIT's my first choice, too," I tell her with a smile.

When she cocks her head at Pascal, he gives us a secretive wink. "Thinking of Stanford."

"Zayd?" Mina queries gently.

Pascal flushes. "Maybe."

And that's when Kimberly decides to ruin our pleasant lunch. Tristan's surges to his feet the moment she approaches our table. I don't stand, but Eric shifts himself so he's sitting on the table and facing the irate girl. If Kimberly wants to get within a foot of Mina, she'll have to deal with four – five if you add Pascal – over-protective assholes.

Midsummer follows like a sullen shadow. "Have you told her, Tristan, all the things you've done? I can't imagine a good girl like Mina would want my sloppy seconds," Kimberly sneers.

"You know, Kimberly," I interject before Tristan blows up, "you reek of desperation. No one at this table wants you." I gesture at Midsummer. "Or you. If you had a smidgen of self-esteem, you'd walk away right now."

"After all that I did to you, he still let me touch him, Mina. He let me s—"

Tristan's there suddenly, his hand clamping around Kimberly's throat hard. I quickly glance around. There aren't any staff present right now, but we have eyes on us.

"Tristan," I warn in a low voice as Kimberly's eyes bulge, but he's beyond listening.

"Tristan, don't." Mina doesn't need to shout. Eric slides over so Mina can address Kimberly directly. Tristan, with a single glance at Mina, let's his hand fall. He's not calm, but only Mina can cut through his rage. "Kimberly, I don't plan on holding every poor decision Tristan's made over his head." Her eyes narrow. "But, if you think for a moment that I'm letting Tristan go, you're wrong. Tristan's mine. The Knights are mine. Heck, even Pascal's mine." Pascal grins at her. "If you cross me, you cross all of them. The converse is equally true. The Steele fortune is at my fingertips. You've found me complacent, but that changes now. *Walk away*." Mina stops to bend her head closer. "We have evidence of what you did. If you think I'm afraid to press charges, think again. I will gladly drag you to hell and back."

Kimberly wavers, but it's Midsummer who bends. Grabbing her friend's hand, she drags Kimberly away.

Tristan swiftly returns to Mina's side, and the look in his eyes makes me wish they could get a room somewhere. "I'm yours?" he asks tenderly, his hand cupping her face.

Her dark eyes sweep over us before settling on Tristan. "Mine," she says with a smile.

Pascal pulls me and Eric aside in the afternoon. He arrived at Mina's party after the revelations. When Mina joined us in the pool, the back of her swimsuit showing the soft lines of scars, he said nothing. He understood, perhaps far more than we would've at one point, that Mina's past is layered with darkness.

"She's doing better," Pascal says to us.

Eric nods. "She's tougher than she looks."

Pascal presses a finger thoughtfully to his lips. "She reminds me of my sister. You guys won't flake out on her again, right?"

It's easy to bristle and be offended. Kai or Tristan would get defensive, which is why Pascal selected us to talk to. "No, we won't. But don't forget about her... or us," I add. "You were there for her when we weren't. We owe you."

Pascal grins. "I know. I may call you on it someday. Until then, it's good to know you have her back."

Tristan texts us. He's dropping Mina off at home since she needs to sign some legal papers, but he wants us to stop by so we can plan our Christmas break. I figure it will also be the perfect time to bring up Sean.

Our initial focus has been Mina. If today is any indication, our fierce little queen is back. I saw the way Kai's eyes glowed, the way Tristan responded to her, the way Eric stood behind her as she faced Kimberly down. I also saw the way Mina looked at Tristan. She may have claimed all of us in that instant, but it's Tristan's heart that she claimed publicly. I strongly suspect Tristan's going to walk around like an arrogant peacock.

All the guys drove separately this morning, so Kai and Eric head straight to Tristan's. As I'm low on gas, I make a pit stop to fill up, running into the convenience store to grab snacks for everyone. Just as I'm ready to head to Tristan's, I swear I think I see Sean in a car. I blink. Sean's at Harvard, and he doesn't come home between semesters. When I look again, I don't see the car. I chalk it up to my imagination.

When I arrive at Tristan's, the guys are in a good mood. I throw the chips on the table. It's good to see Tristan and Kai getting along. Mina's never been one for puppy love, and what Tristan feels for her is as far from puppy love as one can get. Kai's beginning to see that.

"We need to have a massive snowball fight," Eric says with relish after Kai talks about the snowmobiles he'll have ready.

I rap my knuckles on the table. "Look, I hate being grim, but we haven't dealt with Sean yet. We need to take him down. It makes me sick to think he'll graduate from Harvard this year."

Tristan smirks cruelly. "I doubt he'll be able to pay his tuition. Mom froze his trust fund."

At once, we're asking questions. Tristan fills us in that his parents have been covering Sean to protect the family name. After confronting his mother, she agreed to freeze Sean's trust fund. I'm annoyed that Tristan didn't tell us this earlier.

Kai gives Tristan a worried frown. "He's got to be pissed,

Tristan."

"As soon as the semester is over, I'll get a security detail for Mina," Tristan assures us.

But an eerie feeling fills me. "Shit. Maybe it's nothing, but I thought I saw Sean on my way here," I say. I'm starting to wish I spoke up sooner. "But the car wasn't anything fancy, so I thought I was wrong."

Tristan stands abruptly. "You *thought*?" He's already grabbing his car keys while he pulls out his phone.

Tristan messages Mina as Kai slips his jacket back on. "I'm heading over there," Kai announces, but we're already moving to the door.

We freeze as we reach our cars. All our tires are slashed. As fear for Mina creeps up my spine, Tristan's face shifts into alarm. He's running to the main house while calling Mina. I hear him begging her to pick up.

Eric has the sense to call Shin. Shin picks up and Eric moves away from us, talking to him tensely. My heart sinks when I hear Eric say, "What do you mean you didn't ask Mina to come and sign papers?" Eric's green eyes meet mine in terror as Tristan screeches around the corner in his Bentley.

Tristan barely comes to stop for us to jump in before racing towards Steele manor.

Hold on, Mina, we're coming. I curse my stupidity. I should have mentioned it sooner.

Please don't take her from us. I don't realize I say the words aloud until Kai grabs my arm.

CHAPTER TWENTY-SEVEN

When I get home, Shin isn't there. I throw my bag on the table and text him to let him know I'm home. Tristan messages me to tell me the guys are heading to his place for food and I should stop by once I'm done with Shin. I find myself humming a tune.

Shin: *Hey, my car is acting up. I'm in the garage.*

Why Shin doesn't just come inside is beyond me. I tuck my phone in my pocket and make my way there. The garage is dark, and I fumble for the lights, but they don't seem to be working. Suddenly, a hand snakes around my mouth, and something hard digs into my waist.

"What you feel, dear Mina, is a gun. Now, if you want to live, you're going to come with me. Are you going to put up a fight?"

I know that voice. It hasn't changed much since he was eighteen. It's haunted me and plagued me for years. I carefully shake my head and the hand moves away. I face the monster who tried to rape me when I was fourteen.

"Hello, Mina dear," Sean King says with a leer. "Missed me?"

I am desperately glad that the only thing Sean and Tristan have in common is dark hair. Sean's eyes aren't gray. His features are less angular. His lips are thin and severe, not full.

Two thoughts enter my brain. One, I don't want Sean to hurt anyone. If I scream or make a fuss, he'll kill me and probably kill anyone who comes to investigate. Second, he needs to think I'm complacent and afraid. He might relax his guard if I seem meek and terrified.

I don't argue as he forces me outside in the bitter cold and into the driver's seat of his car. He's driving a Honda with out-of-state plates. Either he stole it or borrowed it.

"Where are we going?" I ask, trying to sound timid.

Sean's smile chills my blood. "We're going home, Mina. Back to where it all began."

My shaking hands aren't faked.

The home I lived in for two years with my parents and Shin is for sale. I don't know who bought it after us or if it changed hands, but the home is empty. Sean directs me to the back where my tree fort still stands. Tears prick my eyes as I stare at it for a few seconds. *Please find me.*

Sean, carrying a crowbar, pushes the gun into my back. "Let's go inside and relive our childhood, Mina."

At the back door, Sean swings the crowbar at the glass in the door and gets us inside. "God, brings back memories, doesn't it?" Sean continues conversationally. "Imagine my surprise when Tristan called to tell me he knows the truth. Sure took him long enough, don't you think?"

I'm silent. A few months ago – even a few weeks ago – I wouldn't have cared if he shot me. But I want to live now. I want to know what it's like to be with Tristan. I want to go to college. I want to see my friends get married and have families.

"You two are together, aren't you?" Sean sneers at me. "Have you two done the deed yet?"

I fight down the urge to be sick. "What do you want?"

"Want?" Sean laughs out loud. "Let me see. I want my fucking trust fund released to me. I want to get that video that Tristan has. And I think I want to ruin you. Not necessarily in that order, though."

When I begin to back away, Sean raises the gun. "No, no, don't run away, Mina. I promise you'll never want Tristan again after you've had me."

I close my eyes, steadying myself. Don't be afraid. Don't panic. "I can give you money. The Steele fortune is mine," I state as calmly as possible.

Sean chuckles. "Oh, that's good. Maybe you can beg for your life. Take your clothes off."

There's a decision to be made. Fight or give in. I will shatter if Sean rapes me. There won't be enough of me to put back together emotionally, and it's something I can't do to Tristan or the others. But that doesn't mean I have to fight stupidly.

"Not here," I say. "Not down here. Upstairs. In one of the bedrooms."

Sean's brief confusion clears. "Well, maybe you're a whore, after all. Want to compare who's better, me or Tristan?"

I lick my lips. "Yes. I mean, you're older, so you have more experience." I pretend to check him out. "You look good to boot."

Sean makes this nasty sound. "I don't do gentle. I like it when my girls scream."

I beg my body not to show my revulsion as I move to the stairs. "Let's get on with it," I say.

Sean runs the gun along my face, and I flinch. "You're shaking. You've never been a good liar. But let's go upstairs. I'll enjoy hurting you in your old bedroom."

Climbing the stairs, my knees give out as I start weeping. I scream when he yanks at my hair and orders to keep moving, cowering. Just as he lets go, I see my chance. I kick back as hard as I can, catching Sean in the stomach. The gun goes off, missing me, as he tumbles back. I don't stop to look. I run up the stairs. I'm out of the stairwell when the second shot goes off.

In my former bedroom, I lock the door. It's not going to hold long. I run into the bathroom, locking that door, too, because I remember the bathroom has a window above the screen porch.

I don't pause to think long. I open the window, kicking out the screen. It doesn't take a genius to recognize the sounds of Sean shooting through the door. I crawl onto the ledge before lowering myself, my hands clinging to the window ledge. It will be a drop. Closing my eyes, I let go, hitting the metal roof of the porch. My ankle twists under me, the pain sucking me in, but I begin my mad scramble to get away when I see Sean's head poke out the window.

I roll off the roof and throw myself to chance, disappearing from Sean's line of sight. The snow barely softens the fall as it knocks the wind out of my body. I spasm in pain. Adrenaline fuels me to move, but I can't stand as I'm half-buried in the snow and my ankle won't support my weight. I crawl, using my one good foot to dig in. He'll probably kill me, but at least I won't go down without a fight. I will leave physical evidence everywhere.

Beneath the snow, my hand encounters a rock about the size of my fist. Sean bellows my name as he comes outside. My fingers start to feel numb, but I concentrate as best as I can. I roll on my back, and with as much strength as I can muster, I throw the rock at Sean's face.

It's not hard enough to seriously maim him, but I get lucky in that it hits him in the forehead and distracts him. My reprieve is short-lived.

Sean's on me, and he uses his free hand to slap me hard enough for my ears to ring. I taste blood in my mouth. His hand goes to my throat. When he tries to kiss me, I twist my head and bite his arm as hard as I can, feeling his skin break in my mouth. His hand loosens as he howls. At this point, I'm simply hoping he kills me in rage.

But suddenly, Sean's face goes from anger and pain to surprise as a roar comes from behind him and he's thrown off me. Kai is there, twisting Sean's hand so brutally that I think I hear a bone crack as the gun falls to the ground. Eric grabs the gun while Nate rushes to my side. Tristan looks at me for a second before he growls and tackles Sean, wrestling his brother from

Kai's grasp.

Before Sean can say anything, Tristan's fist slams repeatedly into Sean's face. I can't make out the string of curses Tristan bellows at his brother, but I do hear wet thuds and gurgled sounds of pain from Sean.

"Tristan," I cry, and my voice causes him to freeze. Sean hangs limp, senseless, and bloodied. I'm not sure he even has a face anymore. Tristan flings his brother back in disgust, chest heaving as he stumbles towards me. I hear Eric on his phone, calling the police, as Kai takes another swing at Sean for good measure before flipping the older guy over, straddling him, and pinning his arm down.

Tristan's bruised and bloodied hand reaches for me, but when his gray eyes see Sean's blood on his hand, he wipes it off on his shirt. His knuckles are raw. "Mina, don't move," he croaks, pressing a gentle kiss to my lips. When he lifts his head, I see my blood on his mouth. "You're safe. I'm so sorry, Mina. So sorry. I didn't think, love."

I want to tell him it's okay. But things start to get blurry.

"Mina, stay with me," Tristan pleads, "look at me. Don't close your eyes."

It'd be lovely to obey, but my body has no intention of listening. I'm too hurt. The world winks out of existence.

CHAPTER TWENTY-EIGHT

Tristan

I refuse to leave Mina's side. At the hospital, they determine that Mina has a concussion, a rib fracture, a twisted ankle, and her body is badly bruised. There's no evidence of internal bleeding. She hasn't regained consciousness, which worries me, but the nurse assures me and Shin that considering Mina's injuries, it's normal. I demand second and third opinions, threatening the staff if they miss anything.

What made me think Sean wouldn't lash out when I made Mom cut him off? How many times do I have to screw up where Mina's concerned? I promised to keep her safe. I promised no one would hurt her!

I'd feel better if Shin would yell at me. Instead, he comes periodically to stroke Mina's hair back, barely acknowledging my existence, his eyes in another world altogether. What nightmares plague him when no one is looking?

Right now, my only concern is for the girl before me. I kiss the back of Mina's hand, and tears slip down my cheeks. "Open your eyes, love," I whisper in a broken voice. "I love you. I love you so damn much. I need you to be okay. I told you my love is forever. You're my forever."

Carefully, I lean over her to kiss her forehead gently.

Mina's head shifts slightly. "Mina?" I trace her face gently with a finger, avoiding the bruised areas. "Mina, love, can you hear me?"

Shin moves to the other side as Mina's eyes slowly flutter open. "Hey, sis. I'm going to get the nurse." He looks at me briefly before leaving. I know he can use the call button – he's trying to give us a private moment.

I swallow at Shin's trust in me.

"Tristan." My name is barely a whisper from her lips.

"Sean will never threaten you again," I swear. "They arrested him." God, why would she believe me? I keep failing her.

Mina blinks slowly. "I want to… I want to press charges… when I was fourteen."

Every protective bone in my body wants to scream no when I realize what she's saying. But this is not my decision. It's hers. "Alright, Mina." I kiss her hand again.

The doctor comes in with Shin and a nurse. They go over Mina's vitals, and when she groans, the doctor authorizes additional pain medication.

Mina's eyes start to close after the nurse leaves, but she turns her head to look at me with an unfocused gaze. "Tristan," she whispers.

My heart clenches. "I'm right here," I say as she falls asleep.

The detective takes Kimberly's phone and reviews the video. I've left Mina's side only to get the charges against Sean started. The detective watches the video, her lips pressed thinly in disgust. "With the victim's age at the time, we should be able to add additional charges to his assault. The current district attorney is hard on child predators."

I don't say anything because Kai, Nate, and Eric are pressuring their parents to influence whoever to ensure that Sean suffers appropriately. Technically penniless, he'll need to use a public defender. Sean has been a bully in the outside world only because he's been protected by wealth and privilege. That will be ripped away and he can rot in prison for all I care. If it would bring Mina peace, I'd cut his heart out and serve it to her on a platter.

I hate the word "victim," but since I want to stay on the detective's good side, I don't argue. I don't care about the King name. Sean will pay. Kimberly will burn. And if justice fails, I'll take matters into my hands.

We're the Knights at Broadmoor Prep, but we also come from the more powerful families in town. Mina and Shin haven't exercised their family name yet, but they'll come to understand the strength of the Steele name soon enough.

Going after Kimberly is slightly more difficult. The Moore family has lived here for generations, but they are not well-liked. Since Kimberly is eighteen, I intend for her to be destroyed publicly. I set Eric and Nate in charge of making things happen. I don't want to be gone from the hospital for too long.

When I return, Mina is already awake. I'm annoyed that my mission took so long. Mina's in quiet conversation with Shin, but she's alert enough to ask a dozen questions as soon as I enter.

"Seriously, Mina, you don't need to worry about homework," Shin says in exasperation. "You'll take your semester finals after the new year and they'll adjust your grades accordingly."

"I can take them next week," Mina insists.

"Mina," I growl softly. "Can we at least wait until you get cleared to go home?" I give Shin a look.

"Talking about home, I'm going to head home to shower and clean up," Shin says.

"I'll stay here with Mina," I offer. When she opens her mouth, I add, "I'm not going anywhere."

After Shin leaves, I caress her cheek, relishing the relief of knowing she's conscious and with me. "How are you feeling?" I ask, my fingers itching to delve beneath her gown to check.

"Like I fell off a roof," she says with a slight smile.

I lower my eyes. "I keep apologizing, Mina. I should've known Sean would've come here for revenge. I thought he'd wait until the semester was over. I never expected him to leave school early."

She adjusts the IV line so it doesn't snag on the sheets. "We got distracted. To be honest, I never thought he'd show up the way he did. He cloned Shin's phone."

I cover her hand. "I gave Kimberly's cell to the police."

Mina sighs, wincing when her ribs protest. "I'm not hiding anymore, and I'm not going to let Sean hurt anyone else. I know this will hurt your mom, but I need to press charges. The evidence is circumstantial, but we have the video."

"I'm on board, Mina. We all are." I dip my chin. "When I saw Sean on top of you—" I break off. "I wanted to kill him." I see her eyes linger on my swollen, bloodied, and bruised hand. "I'm okay."

"Are you?" There's no rancor in her voice when she continues, "He's your brother, Tristan. The bonds were strong enough that you believed—"

Each word of hers cuts me like a knife. "I know," I snap, immediately regretting my harsh tone. "I know," I repeat. "I reacted that way because of my insecurities and because I felt guilty for flirting with Kimberly. I have no bonds with Sean. You're my world, Mina." I grimace. "I screwed up so many times. And honestly, I don't have justifiable reasons for them other than plain stupidity and lack of foresight."

Mina pertly says, "That's incorrect."

"What?"

There's a glint in her eyes. "When you're drowning, you don't say 'I would be incredibly pleased if someone would have the foresight to notice me drowning and come and help me,' you just scream." She pauses. "John Lennon said that. You reacted and were reactive in situations where you could have been less so. It doesn't make you a bad person. I did the same thing."

I narrow my eyes at her. "I can't tell if you're making fun

of me or if you're trying to empathize."

Her lips twitch. "Well, then you should think about it. It's probably a mix of both. Oh, and by the way…"

I'm in the process of leaning over to kiss her when I stop. "Hmm?"

The hand without an IV reaches up slowly to caress my face. "I love you, Tristan. I always have."

My breathing hitches as I stare at her for a few seconds. Something in my chest loosens and expands as her words sink it. My head screams, *Don't blow this!* Our kiss starts slow and soft, and I let her drive the pace, getting lost in the feel of her beneath my hands.

"Are you seriously mauling an injured girl, Tristan?" Eric jibes as the other three Knights enter the room.

I flip Eric off, running my tongue along the edge of Mina's lips before scowling at the guys. Kai's dark eyes flicker, but there's no resentment or obvious jealousy in his gaze.

Nate saunters in like he owns the place. He might. His dad invests in a lot of businesses. Pressing a quick kiss on Mina's head, he gently moves her head to look at her face. "I wish I'd hit him, too," he says half to himself.

Mina's lips tremble a bit. She hasn't processed what happened fully and it's taking some time to compartmentalize. "I'd normally tell you that violence doesn't pay—" Her voice cracks with emotion as she averts her head. "Dammit," she whispers to herself, her eyes pinching in discomfort from pain.

I reach for Mina's hand again as Kai comes by Nate. "Don't you blame yourself," Kai states roughly. "You fought. You fought hard enough for us to find you."

"How did you find me?" she asks, lifting her head to look at all of us.

Nate and Kai inch back slowly as Eric admits, "We installed a tracking program on your phone."

"You what?!"

CHAPTER TWENTY-NINE

Recovery is never easy. Whether the injury is physical, emotional, or a mix, it's often two steps forward and one step back. I'm stubborn. I take my finals and ace them while Kimberly Moore is suspended indefinitely and then expelled. No one seems to care about Sean, the poor rich boy, being denied bail. Due to the nature of the crime, and my age when the initial assault occurred, the media keeps a tight lid on my name. It wouldn't surprise me if Nate's family – a power to be reckoned with when it comes to online media – had a hand in that.

Physically, I heal quickly. My ankle remains weak, but since nothing fractured, I'm able to move around easily after a few days. Emotionally, there are moments when I jump at sounds and react poorly at imagined shadows. My dreams are not always peaceful.

We still go to Telluride. To be honest, I think the Knights would have taken me there by force if I refused. The first thing I demand is a tree. The guys want to hit the slopes, but I refuse to release them until we get a tree and decorate.

"Don't cluster the ornaments," Eric scolds Nate. "You're supposed to distribute them evenly."

When the two get into an argument on how to decorate a tree – yes, they use YouTube for advice – Shin and Kai announce they need to get groceries. Tristan drags me off to make cookies.

"I'm not sure this is helping me with cookies," I note as Tristan runs his lips along my neck.

Tristan's been careful about how physical he gets with

me, verifying that I'm comfortable with his touches.

His breath fans against my skin. "I'm double-checking your measurements," he murmurs, angling my head back. "You shouldn't be on your feet this long anyway. Your ankle is still healing." When I scowl, he kisses me until we're both breathless. "You should rest your foot. Do you want to go up to your room?"

I let him carry me to my room before realizing that I'm in his room. When I glance at him questioningly as he lays me on the bed, he says, "I know you're having nightmares, Mina. I'm not letting you sleep alone. I already talked to Shin."

"You told Shin you wanted to sleep with me?" I deadpan.

Tristan's gray eyes are serious. "I told him I wanted to hold you while you slept and be there if a nightmare strikes. He agreed." When I give him a skeptical look, he adds, "With some persuasion on my part. It's creature comfort only."

I run my fingers through his hair. "Just creature comfort?"

Tristan stills above me, his eyes searching mine. "Mina?"

This time I take the initiative to kiss him. "And what if I want something more than creature comfort?" I run my hand down his chest, stopping at the hem of his shirt.

"You only have to ask," Tristan rasps out, his eyes darkening.

"I'm asking," I whisper.

When the Knights entered my life, as our bonds grew, I wanted our friendship to remain the same. They became my surrogate brothers – my extended family filling that hole my mother left – and made me feel loved and wanted. Part of that desire to cling to the past harmed us at times. It made me keep all four of them close – too close, perhaps – and even I know that my actions were selfish. Now that we've established the boundaries of our friendships, I hope it gives Kai, Nate, and Eric the space to grow.

I have what I want now. Tristan as my love, my best friends and brother by my side, the world theoretically at my feet. And yet, if memories could be remade, I would give up my fortune without hesitation to make a good portion of my past disappear. My fear of shadows will likely always linger.

"So serious," Tristan whispers, pulling me against his bare chest.

I tuck myself to his side, running my fingers over his skin. It feels natural to be next to him.

"Are you okay?" he asks when I remain silent, brushing my hair back gently.

I look at him with a smile. "I am." Then I blush when I think about why he's asking me.

With a cocksure grin, Tristan promises, "It gets better." I turn furiously red. He swallows, his heart in his eyes. "This isn't a game, Mina. You and me. I want this to be forever."

Our fingers entwine in a silent promise. "I know. I want that, too."

A sudden knock and the door opens. "Hey, Tristan, have you – holy crap!" Nate shouts.

I dive beneath the covers while Tristan swears. "Shit, I thought the door was locked," Tristan mumbles.

"Oh, my God," Nate says loudly. "You two did it."

I hear Eric in the background. "Who did what?"

"Will you get out of here?" I demand, peeking over the sheet to see Eric join Nate at the door. His green eyes widen.

"How was it?" Eric blurts.

"None of your fucking business," Tristan snaps, his hand trying to calm me down. "Get out and close the damn door before Shin gets here."

Eric starts laughing. "Oh, man. Shin is going to kill you."

They leave and when the door closes, I look at Tristan with wide eyes. "This isn't good."

In the distance, I hear a roar from Shin and wince. Tristan closes his eyes. "Let's get dressed, love, so we can deal with your irate brother."

The other three Knights enjoy Tristan's discomfiture. My brother and Tristan are having an epic staredown. At least, Tristan and Shin haven't come to blows.

Eric hands Nate the popcorn. Kai tries to look apologetic, but he grabs a handful of popcorn and munches away while I glare at them.

"I want to know what you did to get my sister to agree to—" He breaks off and waves between me and Tristan. "You have a rep, King. It isn't a pleasant one. Have you been tested for STDs?" My brother ignores my shriek.

Tristan doesn't blush. "I've used protection every time. And yes, I do get tested. I'm clean, Shin. Do you think I'd put my needs before Mina's health and safety?

"Yes," Eric and Nate say together. Tristan flips them off.

Shin rolls his eyes. "Mina—"

"Don't. Just don't," I state. "I'm eighteen. Stop treating me like a baby."

Nate, Eric, and Kai continue to eat popcorn

Shin scowls.

I cross my arms. "Now if you don't mind, I want to shower and finish the cookies." I glare at the three Knights. "You three are not off the hook either." When they cringe under my thinly veiled anger, I add sweetly, "We need firewood for the fireplace. And guess who volunteered to do the dishes?"

"But we have a dishwasher!" Kai protests.

I don't smile. "I believe in prewashing the dishes. Clean the kitchen up so I can make cookies."

"Need help in the shower?" Tristan asks with a wicked look. Shin looks ready to have an aneurysm.

I blush furiously. "I think I prefer to be alone."

As I leave, I hear Kai say, "You're a damn lucky bastard, Tristan."

Shin adds, "If you hurt her, I'll kill you. And that's after these three beat you within an inch of your life."

CHAPTER THIRTY

Sean lived as a coward and died like one, too. Rather than facing justice, he hung himself when other victims came forward. Mina was not the only one. In her case alone, there was a recording of her assault. Kimberly, running the risk of being disowned completely by her family, accepts a plea deal. Since she was a minor at the time, the justice system goes easy on her. It isn't enough – not for me and not for the other Knights. I intend to destroy her family even though they cut her off.

As promised, I make Mina officially my queen – or our queen since the other Knights need to lay some claim to her. At the Spring Formal, I arrive with Mina on my arm. Kai, Nate, and Eric are also in attendance. We bow only to her. When Pascal brings his date, Zayd, Mina's the first to embrace them. After Kai has a few private chats with several obstinate students, everyone's on board with accepting them as a couple. Mina dances with me first, and I don't care how possessive I look. I reluctantly let Kai, Eric, Nate, and finally, Pascal take a turn with her before reclaiming her. When another student tries to cut in, he backs off as soon as I level him with a murderous glare.

"I told you that you'd change everyone," Pascal says over lunch a week later. "Where are you all going to college?"

"Mina and I got into BIT, so we'll be there with Nate," I say. Mina's having a quiet chat with Eric about something. "Shin's going to BU."

Kai salutes us with a breadstick. "Eric and I will be in the area at BU. We've been talking about getting a house together."

"Freshmen are required to live in the dorms," Nate says, his eyes lingering curiously on Mina and Eric.

I shrug. "We can do both. What are they going to do? Track us?" I can see Nate already thinking of possibilities. "We'll need enough room so we have our own space. Four bedrooms."

"Five," Kai says with a frown. "Six if Shin lives with us."

I already know that Shin plans to live the college life. He's put his life on hold for too long. "Mina and I can share," I say with a devilish grin. This causes Mina to turn and elbow me. "What?" I pull her against me. "I have no intention of letting you sleep alone," I whisper for her ears only. "You sleep better next to me."

I love watching the way her skin flushes. Her dark eyes turn to Eric in encouragement.

Eric gives a nervous smile. "I'm deferring for a year to train for the Olympics," he finally says.

Nate's eyes grow huge as Pascal gives his teammate a high five. "What does this mean about living together, though?" Kai asks.

Eric exhales slowly. "I'll be able to train nearby, so we can still do that. But I'll have to travel a bit, and I hope you'll watch me at key competitions."

"Of course, we will," I say confidently. "Mina would kill us if we didn't support you anyway."

"Are we going to do this?" Mina asks. "Find a place and live together?"

We all nod. "I told you, Mina. You're not getting rid of us," Nate says with a broad wink. "Besides, when Tristan pisses you off, we need to be close by to thrash him."

Eric drapes an arm around Mina. "And console you," he says with a waggle of his eyebrows.

I push his arm off. "Think again, asshole."

Pascal shakes his head. "If the Neanderthal gets too much for you, call me, Mina."

"What are we doing here?" Mina asks in the main lobby of the administration building.

Kai, holding Mina's bag, says, "We're meeting some of the Lower School students."

"Our reign is coming to an end," I say, holding Mina by the waist. "We need to pick the future elite rulers of the school."

Mina scrunches her nose at me. "That's such a snobby tradition. Someone should end it. Why am I here?"

Both Nate and Eric give her a surprised look. "Because you're part of us," Eric says. "The Queen and her Knights."

Just then, a handful of eighth-graders arrive with Pascal. "This is my sister, Shiori. Shiori, this is Mina."

Shiori is a dainty creature with a round face and large eyes. Her smile is genuine. "Mina! I've heard so many wonderful things about you." I release Mina long enough so she can embrace Shiori. The younger girl turns to her friend. "See, I told you there could be a queen."

The girl next to her could be Mina's younger sister except that Mina has double-lidded eyes. But after Shiori's comment, the tall boy next to her scoffs.

"There's only one set of elites. She's with them." The boy's blue eyes wander over Mina appreciatively, noting my hand at her waist. He looks at me and smirks.

This piece of shit is about to get a black eye if he keeps looking at Mina that way.

"We're the Idols. I'm Fox Hemsworth," says the blue-eyed asshole. He brushes his dark blond hair back.

The boy with red-gold hair and hazel eyes dips his chin. "I'm Apollo Vasco."

The dark-skinned boy crosses his arms across his chest. "Chad Keahi."

Mina looks at Shiori's friend. "And you're not with

them?"

"God, no! I'm Wynter Hall. I just started at Broadmoor's Lower School." Her eyes slide to Fox. "When I heard the Idols were coming to meet with the Knights and that there is a queen, I had to see what this was all about."

"Mina's part of the Knights," Apollo snaps, rolling his eyes.

"Correction, she's *the* Queen and we're her Knights," Nate retorts, glaring at the younger boy.

Wynter gives a cold smile. "Just like how I will rule the school, Fox. But unlike them," she says, waving at us, "I intend to rule alone. They can anoint you for all I care. By the time I'm done, the school will forget about the Idols."

Mina hides a smile behind her hand. "You three will have your hands full." Tilting her head at Wynter, she says, "Keep your friends and family close at Broadmoor. The school is full of sharks."

"I like you," Wynter says to Mina suddenly. "You remind me of someone…" A strange look enters her dark eyes. She snaps her fingers, which makes Mina frown. "Come on, Shiori, we've seen enough. Let's go."

Shiori gives her brother an apologetic look. "It was nice meeting you all," she says.

Kai rests his chin on his hand. "You need to get that under control," he says to the Idols. If we're going to pass control of the school to you, there can't be this competition. Either you guys rule or she rules."

Fox frowns. I see echoes of myself in him. "We have it under control," he says. "She's new and thinks she can get away with anything and everything."

I notice the way Chad Keahi continues to look at the door that Wynter has disappeared through. "Mina? Thoughts?"

She laughs. "Oh, no. I'm not getting involved. I think this whole elite thing is stupid. I won't be a party to this."

"Nate? Kai? Eric?" They slowly nod. "Fine. Assuming we don't hear anything that concerns us, we will pass the reigns over to you when we leave." Fox's shoulders relax when he hears my words. "I will give you a bit of advice, though."

The arrogance from Fox is something to behold. "Oh?"

"You'll have the school at your feet if you play your cards right. But there are people out there worth more than the adoration of a school. From one elite to another, be careful who you burn. And most of all, don't burn the one person who is worth having."

My words make the Idols furrow their brows. They're too young to get it now, but it's something I wish I'd known before I hurt Mina the way I did. Forgiveness only occurred because a past connected us.

Mina leans her head against my shoulder. I know she understands where my words are coming from and why I'm saying it now. Her advice is simpler. "Don't be assholes," she adds.

After the three boys leave, I pour on the PDA with Mina, ignoring the muttered groans from Nate and Eric. When she's breathless, I say, "Their school years should be interesting. I don't think that girl is going to back down at all."

Pascal agrees. "Broadmoor does weird things to folks. I wish them the best."

"Enough about them. This is our last year ruling the school," I point out. "Let's make the rest of the year count." I cup Mina's face. I want good memories that shadow the bad ones. I want Sean and Kimberly forgotten – to be so insignificant that no one cares who or what they were.

Mina holds her hand out to the other. I immediately cover hers with mine. One by one, they place theirs on top, including Pascal. "To making memories we want to remember," she says, understanding my thoughts, and her voice sounds like a caress and a promise to my soul.

EPILOGUE

It doesn't surprise me when Eric brings home the gold for America. He doesn't need the endorsements, so post-Olympics, he starts college at BU. He "shares" a room with Kai and Shin, although Shin pretty much has it all to himself. It becomes a party pad for him. That's right – now that Shin knows there's more of us protecting his sister, he's relaxed a bit. Let's just say that some of his parties are not safe for Mina to know about.

It takes some time, but the others do begin to date. I may throw a few girls their way just to be safe. Mina's mine. The other Knights are her friends and they share her affection, but that doesn't mean I want them to lust after her every time she shows up in a swimsuit.

When Mina turns twenty, I make good on my vow to make her a permanent part of my life. We get married right after we graduate with her friends and brother in attendance. When Mina throws the bouquet, Shiori catches it and blushes, her eyes darting to Kai. Mina's the one who tells me that Pascal caught them kissing before the wedding. Shiori, having come off a tumultuous year at Broadmoor, is still recovering from her experiences.

Life is not about happily ever after. It's about experiencing all that comes with living. We have children. We mourn lost friends. We laugh at our follies. We carry each other during times of sorrow. In the middle of the night, when the wind blows hard, she reaches for me, and I'm there. When I wake feeling empty, I reach for her to reassure myself that she's safe and that she is still with me. I hold her so tightly that I don't know where I end and she begins. In the darkness, I lean her back and make love to her, ignoring the world around us. In the light, I kiss each mark and scar as a testament to her strength. When we're together, the world is alive, brighter. It's a world where every caress fills me with hope, and every look is a promise.

ACKNOWLEDGEMENT

There are so many people I want to acknowledge. When writing this book, I listened to a lot of music by BTS and Taylor Swift. Someday, I will make a playlist.

First, my precious family and friends.
> My husband Josh: love and support.
> My two boys: I know I'm a crazy mom. I still love you.
> My college buds: Bruce, thanks for messaging me when I was down and discouraged; David, thank you for letting me speak my mind honestly.
> Nicolle, I am so glad Josh introduced us that day. You are one of the few that never judge me.
> My mother-in-law and father-in-law: thank you for teaching me patience.
> My sister Lorna: weird that I'm writing pseudo-romance novels, right?

Second, thank you to the bigger online community of friends I've made through games:
> Anchor - for reading my notes
> Zero - for having my back and defending me
> Celestikun - we started in one game and still keep in touch
> Kahlan - for teaching me how to use Twitter
> To my guildmates in Guild Leon and my friends in Nightshade - thanks for letting me be weird
> Missy - for letting me cry
> aibretty - for being my panda bear
> Rozz - for loving BTS as much as I do

ABOUT THE AUTHOR

L J Byrne

LJ Byrne lives in the Twin Cities with her husband, two kids, two bunnies, and a very fluffy cat. An engineer by education, a scientist at heart, a writer in her soul, she's had an avid imagination since youth. She's a self-taught speed reader and full of useless facts and information, and her friends call her the female Cliff Claven. She likes  strong female characters who may be put through the wringer but emerge stronger than ever.

https://www.goodreads.com/author/show/20244678.L_J_Byrne

Twitter: www.twitter.com/LJByrne2

BOOKS BY THIS AUTHOR

Survivor

The Betrayal

Turn The Tables

SHATTERED

www.ingramcontent.com/pod-product-compliance
Lightning Source LLC
Chambersburg PA
CBHW071614150726
48000CB00004B/1723